"Let's go," Alex said, hooking her hand through Andrei's arm. She flashed a parting smile at Leah.

Andrei didn't move. "Leah, you come, too." Andrei's smile was warm and inviting, and Leah's heart skipped a beat.

"But Leah has so much to do tonight. We were just talking about that, weren't we?" Alex was smiling, but her eyes were narrowed and Leah got the message.

"Uh—that's right," Leah smiled. "I can't go tonight. Maybe some other time," she said weakly, giving them a little wave as they walked out the door.

"Oh, Alex," Leah murmured under her breath. "What's gotten into you?" Alex might be ready to live with the fact the Leah got the prize part in the gala, but she was not about to share one moment of her precious time with Andrei. Leah didn't know what more she could do or say to convince Alex that she wasn't going to steal her guy—no matter how attractive she was beginning to find him.

CHANGING PARTNERS

Satin Slippers #4

Elizabeth Bernard

FAWCETT GIRLS ONLY • NEW YORK

For Robert Blankshine

RLI: VL 7 & up
      IL 8 & up

A Fawcett Girls Only Book
Published by Ballantine Books
Copyright © 1987 by Cloverdale Press, Inc.

Library of Congress Catalog Card Number: 87-91083

ISBN 0-449-13303-6

First Edition: April 1988

With special thanks to Bonnie August, Freed of London, and Danskin.

Chapter 1

"*Misha!*" Leah Stephenson exclaimed as she climbed the short flight of concrete steps leading to the porch of Mrs. Hanson's boarding-house late one Sunday night. A white paw poked through the narrow opening of Leah's dance bag, followed by the head of an orange-striped kitten. Misha gazed with wide, terrified eyes at the front porch of the three-story house, letting out a plaintive meow at the sound of a foghorn from San Francisco Bay.

"Shhh!" Leah warned, scooping the kitten out of her bag as she fumbled in the dark for her keys. "There's nothing to be afraid of," she assured him. "Mrs. Hanson's boardinghouse is your new home, Misha. Our first stop is the kitchen, to get you some milk."

A car honked at the curb. Leah turned around and waved good-bye to Mr. Dryer, a friend of her mother's, who had driven her back to San Francisco from her hometown of San Lorenzo, California. Pushing her long blond hair out of her eyes, she watched as the car pulled away. Leah paused

a moment after the taillights disappeared around
the corner, thinking how strange it was to come
back to San Francisco, thinking of it, rather than
San Lorenzo, as her real home.

The foghorn wailed again, and Misha dug his
claws into Leah's long handwoven scarf and bur-
ied his face in her hair. "I understand," she whispered into his ear. The foghorn made such a cold,
desolate sound—she had almost forgotten how
lonely it had made her feel when she first heard
it.

She had been living there for just a few months
now, ever since she'd been accepted as a first-
year student at the San Francisco Ballet Academy, official school of the Bay Area Ballet company.
When Leah had first arrived at the school, the
exhilarating routine of almost nonstop dance
classes coupled with a demanding academic schedule exhausted her. Those first nights she was so
tired, she'd lie awake in her bed, every muscle in
her body aching. Too keyed up to sleep, she
would ponder the problems of new friendships,
strange rivalries, and a million new dance steps.
Her exciting new life would shrink down until it
seemed far less glamorous and exciting than she
had thought. She'd get very homesick, for her
mother, her best friend Chrissy, her dog Pavlova,
and Misha. She even missed the dusty, dry air of
the inland valley town and the small but familiar
Main Street dance studio run by her dear teacher,
Hannah Greene. It had seemed so comfortable
and predictable dancing with Miss Greene. It made
her wonder—was it really worth it coming here?

She laughed to herself, remembering her doubts.
Now she wouldn't give up her life at the San

Francisco Ballet Academy for all the money in the world. In spite of a few rude awakenings about life on-stage, Leah was sure she was living the life that was meant for her. To be a dancer had always been Leah's dearest wish, her most cherished dream. And thanks to this school, it was beginning to come true. Tonight the cry of the foghorn seemed to welcome her back to her real home; but it still had the power to make her feel alone in a way she'd never felt before.

The feeling had nothing to do with homesickness now. The problem was her best friend back in San Lorenzo, Chrissy Moreley. This past weekend had been Leah's first visit home since September. Though it had only been a few months, Chrissy had changed—not in a growing-apart sort of way. If anything, Leah felt closer than ever to her childhood buddy. Chrissy had changed because she had fallen in love, the object of her affection being Otto Rabinski, the boy next door. Chrissy was almost as surprised about it as Leah. He was the very same gawky, goofy boy Leah and Chrissy had hung out with from the time they were in the second grade. Now, when Chrissy mentioned his name, her face assumed a silly expression, and her brown eyes took on a soft glow. Leah was very happy for her friends, but their romance made her feel lonely in a way she never had before. Leah couldn't help but wonder if her dancing career would prevent her from ever having a guy.

That's why she had brought Misha back with her—to keep her company. Misha squirmed in her arms and mewed piteously. Leah realized she was hugging him too tight and that the poor little creature hadn't had anything to eat or drink in over two hours. She lifted him up in front of her face, staring into his yellow eyes. "You must be starved! Let's get you that milk!"

Leah unlocked the door and walked in. The wallpapered hallway was bathed in soft light from a table lamp. Mrs. Henson always left it burning all night, in case one of the girls came in late or craved a midnight snack. She checked her watch and groaned softly under breath. Eleven P.M. She'd made Sunday-night curfew by the skin of her teeth.

As she tiptoed further down the hall, Misha clung to her shoulder for dear life and purred at full volume in Leah's ear. His stiff little whiskers tickled her, and Leah giggled out loud. Quickly she looked around. To her right the parlor was dark, and no light seeped from beneath the door of Pamela Hunter's sun-porch bedroom. Leah breathed a sigh of relief; at least she hadn't awakened Pam. The idea of confronting her less-than-pleasant housemate at this hour didn't appeal to Leah. To the left lay the kitchen. Leah set her bag down softly at the foot of the stairs and, whispering sweet nothings to the kitten, pushed open the swinging door leading to the kitchen. She gasped at the strange sight that met her eyes. The kitchen was illuminated by candlelight, and shadows danced among the gleaming pots and pans hanging on the wall. Two figures sat huddled over the Formica-top table peering into a mug, unaware of Leah standing in the doorway.

"Hello there!" said the young man, looking up. He spoke with a heavy yet familiar accent. In the uncertain light, Leah couldn't make out the color of his thick, wavy hair.

The other figure spun around. Much to Leah's surprise, it was Alexandra Sorokin, a third-year student at the school and one of Leah's best friends. Alex jumped to her feet and whipped her long black hair out of her eyes. Leah stared at her friend—she'd never seen Alex wear her hair down before. The dramatically dark Russian girl looked even more beautiful—and somehow older—than usual. She definitely didn't look happy to see Leah.

"Uh ... hi, Leah. What are you doing here?" Alex asked, in the same accent as the young man. She sounded nervous, as if she'd been caught off guard, not at all like her usual coolheaded, confident self.

"What am *I* doing here?" Leah stumbled over her words. She looked from Alex to the young man and back to Alex again. It was past curfew, and Alex was sitting alone in a candlelit kitchen with a guy. She waited for Alex to give some kind of explanation.

The young man broke the silence. "Is that a baby cat?" he asked. A moment later he had crossed the room and was standing by Leah's side. Even in the dark she could see he moved like a panther. Leah instantly recognized his dancer's build and walk. But she had a sense that he wasn't just any dancer—he must be a rather exceptional one. He reached over her shoulder and flicked on the overhead light. The sudden fluorescent glare made Leah blink. When she opened her eyes again she found herself looking up into eyes as blue as her own.

"May I please pet your cat?" he asked, a shy smile lighting up his face.

"Sure," Leah replied, looking over his shoulder and once again meeting Alex's eyes. Why didn't Alex explain what was going on here, especially the identity of her good-looking friend?

Alex returned Leah's stare but didn't smile. A tiny frown creased her high forehead as she shifted her gaze to the man. He was very close to Leah now, murmuring baby talk to the cat. Misha understood him, even though he was not speaking English. The kitten stretched out his paws and jumped confidently into the stranger's arms.

The man laughed with pleasure, and keeping his eyes on Misha, introduced himself. "My name is Andrei Levintoff."

Leah could barely restrain a gasp. Only four months ago Andrei Levintoff's name was headline news. He had defected from the Kirov Ballet while they were touring Italy, having sought asylum at the American embassy in Rome. Since then he had been guesting with various companies in the States as well as abroad. What in the world was he doing in Mrs. Hanson's kitchen?

Before Leah could ask, he went on to explain, "I dance with the Bay Area Ballet this season, and I teach a course for students at the school, too." He finally looked up from petting the cat and offered Leah his hand.

She stared at the strong, square hand a moment before taking it. She was suddenly conscious of how good-looking he was, and so very sophisticated. He wasn't like the American guys she'd met, she thought as she shook his hand. Touching him was pleasant, but somehow she felt confused, so she dropped her hands to her sides, then clutched them nervously behind her back. "I'm Leah Stephenson. I'm a first-year student at the school." She fell silent, unsure of what to say next. She couldn't take her eyes off of Andrei. Gradually the connection between Andrei and Alex began to make sense. "Did you know Alex's parents at the Kirov?" she asked.

Alex broke in. "He was a student at the school back home. Andrei and I have known each other a very long time." Alex started across the room to join them, but before she could get very far, Andrei invited Leah to the table for tea.

Leah hesitated. Andrei's invitation was warm, and she'd love to have a chance to talk to him, but Alex had caught her eye and did *not* look pleased at Andrei's invitation.

Andrei marched back to the table and pulled out a chair for Leah, continuing Alex's story. "The Sorokins are my friends. I haven't seen Alex for a very long time. Mrs. Hanson said we had a lot to talk about. That is why I am here now, so late." His grin was disarming. Leah found herself smiling and nodding back at him as if he had said something very important. He pulled up a chair and straddled it, reaching over to grab a mug while he motioned for Leah to sit down. "I have known little Alex here since she was just a baby," he said with an affectionate glance at Alex.

Alex cringed and wailed, "Andreiiiii, I wasn't a baby. I was eleven then."

"Ah, yes ..." He paused to tousle Alex's hair, draping his arm around her shoulder. With the other hand he continued to stroke the kitten's thick orange fur. Misha liked Andrei, Leah realized as he began purring loudly, and she could certainly understand why.

"At eleven years you were a grown-up, no?" He chuckled amiably, then turned and winked at Leah as if they shared some kind of secret joke, making her very uncomfortable. Alex didn't seem to want her here, and Andrei's suggestion that they were allies in teasing Alex would just make matters worse. Leah shifted slightly in her chair, edging away from Andrei. She looked helplessly toward Alex. Just then Andrei leaned over and whispered confidentially but loud enough for Alex to hear, "In Russia we think girls of fifteen are still babies."

"I'm seventeen, Andrei Levintoff!" Alex retorted, and actually blushed.

Leah felt her own face redden and wished the kitchen were still just lit with candles—or that she weren't just fifteen. When she glanced up, Alex was looking at her as if she had never seen her before, her large, almond-shaped eyes narrowed. She looked so suspicious of Leah that, after a moment's alarm, Leah burst out laughing. She reached across the table and playfully prodded Alex's arm. "I can't imagine Alexandra Sorokin ever being a baby," Leah said truthfully. Alex was the most grown-up seventeen-year-old she'd ever met.

Alex beamed at Leah's comment, and all shadow of suspicion vanished from her exquisite face. "So we get to meet Misha at long last," Alex said, pulling her chair closer to Andrei and scratching the kitten behind its ears as it dozed in the crook of Andrei's arm. She looked up at Andrei through her thick, dark lashes and continued, "Leah's been home for the weekend. Mrs. Hanson said we could

use a cat, so she brought him back with her."
Alex smiled benignly at Leah. "She named him
after Baryshnikov. He's her favorite male dancer."

For some reason Leah's first impulse was to
deny it, but Andrei didn't give her a chance.

"He is?" he said with a tinge of professional
jealousy in his deep voice. He didn't bother to
wait for Leah to answer. "Is this an American
custom? To name a kitten after someone you
like?" He paused thoughtfully. "If I dance here a
long time, will people name their cats after me?"

His second question took Leah off guard. He
sounded so serious and interested. She giggled
nervously. "I don't know about our customs. But
Misha is very graceful for a kitten—I think of
him as a dancer." The more Leah said, the more
awkward she felt. It was definitely time to change
the subject.

"Why did you light all these candles?" she asked.
No one had bothered to blow them out, even
though now the lights were turned on. Alex smiled
a secret sort of smile, and the situation became
clear to Leah. Suddenly Alex's air of suspicion,
her loose hair, and her anger at being called a
baby all began to make sense. Alex had a crush
on Andrei. Leah felt she should have realized it
earlier. Alex's stories about Andrei came back to
her—how they were friends back in Leningrad,
and how glad Alex was when he defected to the
West. When Alex was a little girl at the Vaganova
Institute, she had faithfully left flowers in front of
his locker every single day for a week, hoping
he'd notice her—but she'd been too scared to
leave a note. So he never knew who they were
from. Apparently Alex's crush had weathered sev-

eral years' separation. Now Leah wished she hadn't asked about the candles. Alex had obviously lit candles to create a romantic setting. To make it up to Alex, she decided to make a hasty exit.

But Andrei's explanation of the candles surprised Leah. "My grandmother told me always to use candles when I read tea leaves," Andrei explained with a charmingly boyish smile. "When I lived at home as a little boy, before I left for the ballet school in Leningrad, my grandmother taught me how to read tea leaves. It was a long time ago, but I will try to do it right." He gave Alex an apologetic yet amused look. "What if I give you the wrong future?" Alex laughed at the mock seriousness of his expression. Andrei turned to Leah, his blue eyes all innocence. "Do you want me to read your tea leaves, Leah?"

"It is getting late," Alex pointed out, giving Leah a meaningful look.

"Uh, yes, and I'm tired and—"

Andrei didn't let Leah finish. "Reading the tea leaves takes no time at all." He jumped up and flicked off the kitchen lights. He rubbed his hands together, his face beaming with expectation. He picked up Leah's mug and dumped the cold remains of her tea into a glass, leaving just a tiny bit of liquid in the bottom of the cup. "We will begin now," he said.

Leah squirmed in her chair, glancing at Alex, whose arms were folded tight against her chest. Candlelight flickered on Alex's dark hair and sculpted face, causing shadows to disguise her expression, yet Leah could see she was not very pleased. Leah cleared her throat and said quickly, "Please read Alex's leaves first. I—I'm not sure I want to hear mine. I'm very superstitious. . . ." She stumbled a little over her lie—everyone, including Alex, knew she was one of the few girls at the Academy who didn't believe in rabbits' feet, four-leaf clovers, or reading the daily horoscopes in the paper.

Andrei began to interrupt, but Alex spoke up. "She is right, Andrei. I go first; then she will see there is no danger in your reading the leaves."

"As you wish," Andrei said obligingly. "To me it is all the same." He shrugged and picked up Alex's cup. He swirled the liquid around, then dumped it into a glass. He put the cup down on the table and peered into it. Alex bent her head close to Andrei's. Leah quickly followed suit. Though she would never have admitted it to a soul, she was truly curious. Yet, Leah was disappointed after one glance at the leaves. She wasn't sure what she had expected to see, but certainly something more than globs of moist brown tea leaves. Peeking up at Andrei through her lashes, Leah saw that his handsome face was set in a serious, intent expression. Shifting her gaze to Alex, she almost laughed. Alex sat poised, without breathing, waiting for Andrei to begin, her dark eyes riveted to the bottom of the cup.

"I see here a journey," Andrei began. "By plane," he added quickly. "To a faraway place. But it will not happen for a long time, and maybe this journey is not for you. No, it is not. People you will love will take a journey away from you."

Alex emitted a frightened gasp, clutching Andrei's arm. "My parents, Andrei, my parents! Soon, they are going far away." She looked up at him, her face full of wonder.

"You mean on that tour of the Far East?" Leah asked, unable to keep the amusement out of her voice. Alex's parents were very famous dancers who traveled the world, guesting with various major companies. Just yesterday Alex had mentioned the possibility of their passing through town soon en route to Japan. "Really, Alex," Leah said doubtfully. She couldn't help thinking that Alex was acting very silly about this fortune-telling, as if Andrei's reading was scary and foreboding news.

"I did not know they go to Far East!" Andrei defended himself, looking from Alex to Leah.

"Don't pay attention to her," Alex grumbled. She shook Andrei's arm. "Is there more?"

Leah tapped her feet together impatiently under the table. She just couldn't wait to hear what else Andrei would make of the messy heap of leaves. She hid her face with her hands and studied the contents of the cup. If she met Alex's eyes, she would burst out laughing for sure.

Andrei peered into the cup, turning it first to the right, then the left. "I see here that someone in this house will fall in love soon. A stranger will come here and change her life."

Alex caught her breath.

Leah looked right at Alex, who began to get a dreamy look in her eyes. Just like Chrissy's smile when she talked about Otto, Leah thought. Alex lowered her lashes and whispered, "Oh, Andrei. My future—is that all there is?"

Andrei laughed. "The future for someone in this house. Yes," he said. "And now you?" He turned to smile at Leah. She felt a pleasant little shiver up and down her spine, and she allowed herself to bask in the unfamiliar feeling. Then suddenly she caught herself and sat up very straight in her chair. Alex wanted to be alone with Andrei. She did not belong there.

"Shall I look at your future?" he asked again. This was the perfect opportunity to leave them alone. Thinking quickly, she pushed her hair back from her face and stifled a make-believe yawn. "I don't think so," she said, stretching her arms and trying to look sleepy. She reached for Misha. He was curled up on Andrei's lap, asleep. "Like I said, I'm a very superstitious person. . . ." Leah gave what she hoped was a convincing little shiver. "You were right about Alex's parents. I'm afraid to hear my future. What if you predicted something I'd rather not know?"

"I am sure I could predict only good things in your future, Leah. But I am happy to have met you," Andrei said, smiling. Before she could become hypnotized by his enchanting blue eyes, Leah turned to leave. Pausing only long enough to pour some milk from a pitcher in the refrigerator into a bowl, she hurried out of the kitchen.

With the door closed safely behind her, Leah leaned against the wall and silently let herself laugh until she thought her sides would split. She never thought she'd see the day cool, sophisticated Alex had a crush. Still grinning, she somehow managed to maneuver her bag, Misha, and the milk into a comfortable position before starting up the steps.

Chapter 2

"Sorokin! What's been going on in that kitchen?" A hoarse whisper floated down from the landing above. "Tell me all about it, right now. I want every single detail. Did he—"

"Katherine Larkin, is that you?" Leah interrupted, pretending to be surprised. She knew perfectly well that no one else but Kay would be waiting halfway up the stairs, ready to waylay Alex and pump her for information about Andrei. Kay was the San Francisco Ballet Academy's self-appointed one-girl grapevine and a good friend of Leah's. She had a nose for news and had come to pride herself on being the first girl in the know about *everything* worth knowing at the school. Her part-time job in the school office and her popularity with the staff kept her informed about every savory bit of company and ballet world gossip that happened to make its way into the Academy. The fact that Alex was in the kitchen *after curfew* with Andrei Levintoff had the makings of a headline story.

"Leah?" Kay questioned, sounding disappointed.

Then she poked her head over the banister. "Ooooh!" she shrieked, spotting the cat's bright golden eyes. "You must be Misha! I've heard a lot about you," Kay said, smiling at Leah. She padded down the stairs and took the bowl of milk from Leah, who was balancing it precariously in one hand. Kay grabbed Leah's elbow and practically dragged her up to the second floor. "I can't believe Alex is still in there with him. It's almost midnight! Wait until you hear what's going on! You're never going to believe it. Alex is in love!" she announced in a loud whisper.

"In love?" Leah repeated skeptically. What she had seen in the kitchen just now hadn't seemed to be love—it was more like a crush. Kay didn't say another word; instead, she steered Leah down the hall to her room. Light streamed out of the open door, along with laughing voices.

"Look what the cat dragged in!" Kay cried, pulling Leah into the room and carefully setting Misha and the milk down on the floor. She drew herself up to her full height of just five feet, and pointing to Leah, she announced, "*She* was inside," she said, pausing dramatically, "with *them!*"

Leah flashed an uncertain smile at the other girls in the room, not sure how she felt about gossiping about her best friend. Melanie Carlucci, Kay's roommate, was there, ankles propped up on the desk, darning the toes of her pointe shoes. Suzanne Winters was sitting cross-legged on Melanie's bed, a loose-leaf binder in her lap. The only boarders not present were Pamela, who was not on friendly terms with Leah or any of her crowd, and Abigail Handhardt, Pam's buddy.

Melanie looked up from her darning and greeted

Leah with a warm smile. "What's going on down there, Leah? The suspense is killing us—or at least some of us!" she said, giving Kay a meaningful look. She reached over to pet the kitten. "Now, aren't you the cutest thing going," Melanie said, stroking his soft fur. Turning again to Leah, she asked, "Does he scratch?"

"No, not at all. Misha loves people," Leah replied, glad to have a moment to pull her thoughts together. Laughing alone outside the kitchen about Alex's crush didn't make her feel disloyal to her friend. But getting entangled in a rap session certainly did. What if Alex regarded it as a highly private matter? Hoping to change the subject, she peeled off her jacket and tossed it on a chair already piled high with Kay's clothes. She said brightly, "I'm glad to see our new mousetrap making himself right at home. I promised him he'd be happy here at Mrs. Hanson's."

She plopped herself down in the middle of Kay's fake-fur throw rug and stretched out her aching legs. She slowly bent forward, letting her forehead come to rest on her knees. She luxuriated in a long sigh, hoping to get some sympathy from the other girls and to keep Kay from asking any more questions. Just as she was about to launch into a very long description of exactly how awful it felt to be crammed into the front seat of a Corvette in heavy weekend traffic, with a two-and-a-half-pound kitten wriggling in your bag, howling his lungs out, Kay cleared her throat loudly. Leah peered up at Kay through her bangs.

Kay's round freckled face was set in a determined expression. She obviously had no intention of being sidetracked from her investigation. Stepping right over Leah where she lay sprawled on the rug, she marched to her bed and sat down beside a heap of pink tights in various stages of disrepair. She ran a hand impatiently through her wild, curly black hair and asked directly, "Out with it, Stephenson. What is Alex up to in there? And what do you think of Andrei?"

Leah remembered how nice Andrei's hand had felt when she shook it, and how blue his eyes were, but for Alex's sake she tried to be noncommittal. "He seems nice...."

Suzanne howled with laughter. She thumped the bed with one hand and shoved her oversize tortoiseshell glasses up on her slender nose with the other. "Nice! I'd say he's the most adorable thing to hit the school since James Cummings!"

Inwardly Leah agreed. Dark, devastatingly handsome James had been her partner until his failure to report a leg injury got him expelled from the Academy. James, however, had not only survived his disgrace but had furthered his career; in another month or so he'd be joining the Joffrey Ballet in New York. None of the other boys who attended SFBA were quite as talented or goodlooking as James.

Melanie looked up from petting Misha and said pointedly to Suzanne, "Andrei Levintoff is *not* in the same class as James. He's already a professional dancer, not a student. He's going to work here as a teacher, as well as perform with the company. He's a big star!"

"That has nothing to do with how cute he is," Kay said, "or with how *interested* he is in Alex."

"Interested is not the word for it!" Melanie

chuckled. "He couldn't get his eyes off of her in class today."

"Madame Preston even said something about it!" Suzanne added, sounding slightly awed.

Kay nodded enthusiastically. "During class we are to watch the teacher, not the other students— she looked directly at Andrei while she spoke. He got the port de bras mixed up, probably because he was so entranced by Alex."

Leah tried to discount this information. Somehow it just didn't jibe with what she had witnessed in the kitchen. Love couldn't be the real explanation. "He hasn't seen her dance since she was eleven," Leah pointed out. "You have to admit, Alexandra is really something to watch in Madame's class." Somehow the young man Leah had just met didn't act like someone in love. "They are old friends," she added, stressing the word "friends."

Kay balled up her pillow and threw it at Leah. "Alex certainly doesn't think of him as just a friend."

"Unless it's convenient," Suzanne remarked. "If Andrei Levintoff hadn't been an old family friend, there's no way Mrs. Hanson would make an exception to the rule about eleven o'clock curfew. Why, it's almost midnight now."

At that moment, Alex burst into the room, just in time to catch Suzanne's last words. "And Cinderella has returned from the ball!" She wrapped her long arms around her chest and hugged herself, then threw them wide open in a joyful, expansive gesture. She stepped into a long, sensuous arabesque; then she executed a few pas de chats, vaulting over a pile of books before landing at the foot of Kay's bed. She looked around the room and returned the girls' smiles, then sat down primly on top of Kay's haphazardly folded quilt. The radiant Alexandra Sorokin looked like Princess Di waiting to be interviewed.

But it was Alex who fired the first question—at Leah. "So, what did you think? Everyone else already met Andrei in Madame's class today."

Leah tried to answer truthfully yet diplomatically. "He seems really nice. I like him. It'll be fun having him as a teacher." Before Leah could ask exactly what he would be teaching, Alex jumped up and gave her a hug.

"I knew you would. I really did." Alex's smile seemed to erase the shadows that always lingered in the corners of her face.

Leah didn't quite know how to respond. Alex's reaction made her feel a bit dishonest. She hadn't liked Andrei in quite the way Alex thought. She kicked off her flats and tugged up the tie-dyed ankle socks she wore over her black tights. She decided it was best not to say anything else about her impressions of Andrei.

"Leah, did you tell them about how he read my tea leaves?"

"Uh, no, not really. I kind of thought that was private and— "

"Andrei reads tea leaves," Alex interrupted Leah.

"Like they do in that crazy Gypsy restaurant down by the pier?" Melanie asked, leaning in a little closer to hear better.

"I do not know that place." Alex shrugged her shoulders. "But he knows the old way we do it in Russia. He learned to read the leaves from his grandmother when he was a young boy."

Kay clasped her hands together eagerly. "So what did he predict?" she asked.

Alex smiled secretively. "Well ..." She hesitated, swinging her long legs back and forth in anticipation. "He told me a handsome stranger is in my future."

"Oh, how wonderful," Kay said, very impressed.

Leah looked up at the ceiling. "Alex, that is *not* exactly what he said."

"It is what he meant, don't you think?" Alex said with a careless shrug. She toyed with the heavy silver pendant that dangled from her neck, and smiled dreamily.

"I don't know what he meant. He simply said, 'Someone in this house will fall in love soon, and a stranger will come and change her life.'"

"So what is the difference?" Alex challenged Leah.

Leah was determined not to give in to Alex's fantasy. Though Alex might think she was just being obstinate, Leah cared about her friend very much. "You heard what you wanted to hear. All fortune-tellers know that. They predict something that could be true for—" Leah gestured vaguely around the room "—for any one of us here. You seem so certain that it's the gospel truth concerning your future—I just wouldn't want to see you get hurt."

"He's not a fortune-teller." Alex exclaimed. "He just knows how to read leaves. Why should he lie or make things up? He's a very good friend of mine."

Leah strove to smooth Alex's ruffled feathers. "I'm not saying he's lying." She tucked her legs under her. "Reading tea leaves is a game," Leah said firmly. "I just think you are taking it too seriously."

"Well, I'm not so sure." Kay stood up for Alex. "Not at all. I believe in tarot cards, palm readings horoscopes, and fortune cookies!" Kay ticked off points on her fingers as she spoke.

Melanie burst out laughing. "You had me pretty convinced until you threw in the fortune cookies. Really, Kay, no one takes them seriously."

"I do," Kay insisted. "Before my mother turned up here last month, a fortune cookie I got at Wo Hops said a stranger would come into my life and turn it around. Lynne Vreeland turned up, and my life certainly won't ever be the same."

Leah was relieved that her friend could talk openly about what had happened between herself and Miss Vreeland. The Ballet Canada star had recently come to San Francisco on tour. Kay had begun to seem strange and withdrawn. To the surprise of everyone but Kay, Lynne Vreeland proved to be her natural mother; Lynne had divorced her husband when Kay was only about a year old. Kay's stepmother had been the only real flesh-and-blood mom she had ever known. While Ballet Canada was in San Francisco, Leah had brought mother and daughter face-to-face. It had been a rocky time for Kay—Leah was proud of how she had come to terms with having, as she put it, "two real moms."

"That fortune cookie was just a coincidence," Melanie pointed out to Kay.

"I do not think so," Alex broke in. "Just like it is no coincidence that my tea leaves talk about a handsome stranger, just when Andrei comes to town. I could tell he knew he was the stranger—

just from the way he said it," Alex concluded, her voice far away.

"You can't be serious!" Leah said, aghast. "Alex, I don't think you should get so carried away with him."

Alex narrowed her eyes and viewed Leah critically. "Why not?" she said, sounding very defensive.

"Because ..." Leah couldn't quite come up with any good reasons now, but she was sure Alex was about to let herself in for a big fall. Suddenly she remembered something. "Because I read in the paper that he's a bit of a flirt."

"Nonsense," Alex said huffily. "You cannot believe those gossip columnists. A new ballet star turns up on the international scene, and they make everything he does, everyone he talks to, into some kind of scandal. Leah, I do not see how you can believe such nonsense."

"It's no more nonsense than tea leaves," Leah said firmly, desperate to save Alex from her dangerous illusions.

"Listen," Alex said, leaping to her feet. "I came to share my good news with friends, not to be ridiculed. If you don't want to hear about Andrei, I will stop talking about him now and do you all a favor."

"Alex," Kay wailed. "I want to hear all about him, really I do." She shot Leah an angry look. "And I, for one, would *love* to have him read my tea leaves."

"That would be so exciting!" Suzanne added.

Alex ignored their comments. With a proud toss of her head and a lingering glare at Leah, she said rather dramatically, "It is late and I am tired. I want to be alone!" With that, she picked her way across the littered floor and walked out the open door, slamming it closed behind her with a bang.

"Oh, boy," Leah said dismally. "I didn't mean for her to get so upset. It's just that she's confusing her expectations of Andrei with his predictions. He didn't say anything definite about *her* love life."

"You only spent a couple of minutes in the kitchen with them, Leah. How do you know what he feels?" Kay said, still irritated with Leah for causing Alex to leave before she could get the story straight.

Melanie quickly intervened. "She can't know what he feels, but Leah's right. Alex is overreacting a bit. Though I do think Andrei likes her."

Suzanne took off her glasses and stuffed them in her bathrobe pocket. "You were a bit hard on her, Leah. I think there is a good chance that Andrei and Alex will get together."

"I didn't mean to be hard on her. I didn't think she'd be that touchy. Alex is usually so ... independent."

"On the other hand," Kay mused, "maybe you're right to worry about her. After all, exactly what did Andrei read in her tea leaves?"

"Oh, some nonsense about a stranger coming along and changing the life of a girl who lives in this house," Leah said impatiently, looking for Misha. The kitten had vanished, and Leah was determined to retrieve him as quickly as possible so she could go up to her room. Like Alex, she wanted to be alone, and she was getting very tired of this discussion.

"That's the point," Kay declared. "When he read

Alex's tea leaves, he said a stranger would come, and he's no stranger to Alex."

"What do you mean?" Suzanne asked.

Kay spelled it out for her, "Andrei's an old friend of Alex's, not a stranger. Don't you see? Leah's right. Alex is in love with Andrei, but a different guy will come along and change her life. Someone she hasn't met yet."

Leah couldn't restrain herself. She scrambled to her feet, exclaiming, "Larkin, you're nuts!" She fished Misha out of Kay's laundry basket. "This fortune-telling is for the birds. I think Alex has gone overboard about this guy—that's all there is to it. She's always had a crush on him, and now she thinks that because she's older, it's turned into love. Well, I, for one, am not convinced."

With that, Leah turned on her heels, picked up her dance bag, and headed out the door. She was careful not to slam it behind her, but as she headed up the stairs to the third floor she began to wonder if everyone in the boardinghouse had gone a little crazy. Everyone was taking Andrei's tea leaves so seriously. Andrei was in a strange country, and his English wasn't great yet. Maybe reading tea leaves was just his way of relating to people, some kind of party game. Remembering his smile, Leah thought that he did seem a little shy.

What surprised Leah was Alex's going overboard like that, falling for the fortune-telling and candlelight as if it were a proven, scientific approach. Not to mention that Andrei hadn't said anything very specific about Alex at all. Just that someone in the boardinghouse would meet a stranger. But Alex was being so headstrong that she had turned Andrei's words around as if they applied to her. Why, he could have meant me! Leah thought. He had wanted to read her tea leaves as well. Or Kay, or anyone else in the house for that matter. And he didn't say that he was the stranger. But obviously Alex hadn't interpreted it that way. Sensible, down-do-earth Alex wasn't the sort to fall in love as though she were falling headlong into a swimming pool. She could take care of herself—or could she? Leah silently wondered.

The thought of Alex being out of control made her smile. As she opened the door to her room, she said to Misha, "And what do you think of Andrei? Will he be true to Alex? Is this love?" But the kitten just stared back at her wide-eyed, unable to tell Leah what the outcome of all this would be.

Chapter 3

When am I going to learn to keep my big mouth shut? Leah wondered the next afternoon. She was exploring the greenhouse, one of the remnants of the ballet academy's prouder days as a private mansion. She stopped to sniff a remarkably gaudy red flower that looked like a tutu with too many layers of tulle. It didn't have any smell, but Leah hardly noticed. She went through the motions of examining the labeled plants, knowing she was there only to kill time before this afternoon's repertory class. If she arrived early, she'd be put in the position of having to talk to Alex. And she had a funny feeling that Alex had decided they weren't talking.

Leah proceeded down the white gravel path back toward the entrance. She kicked a stone hard with her toe, sending it skimming down the walkway until it landed with a click against the metal base of one of the greenhouse tables. Leah hated it when she and Alex were having an argument. When all was said and done, Alex was Leah's best friend here at the Academy, though it was just a couple of months since they had first met. Alex was the person Leah laughed, cried, and joked with the most. Who else but Alexandra Sorokin would have thought of that crazy gag they had pulled on Halloween morning. Leah grinned at the memory of their arriving late at Madame's class in get-ups that even amused Madame. They had worn baggy Victorian bloomers and camisoles over their tights, and they had tied up their hair in a dozen goofy braids, each one fastened with a different color ribbon. Madame had made each of them stand in the front row for centre work and, with a straight face, had insisted that each girl in turn demonstrate fouettés for the class.

Alex had also nursed her through her troubles with James. Leah had grown to depend on Alex's guidance and wisdom, which only an older student at SFBA could possess. Alex was the one person at SFBA that Leah knew she could trust— they were up-front and honest with each other in the way that only good friends can be. And, ironically enough, that's what always caused their problems—Alex was the one friend Leah always fought with. Though she certainly hadn't meant to start an argument over Andrei last night.

Leah tore a sprig of mint off a bushy potted plant by the door and munched it thoughtfully. She hadn't meant Alex to take her criticism of Andrei's tea-leaves reading so hard. But apparently love changed a person. Alex seemed much more touchy and sensitive than usual—not at all like herself. She had interpreted Leah's concern as an attack on Andrei.

Leah wasn't surprised that morning when Alex

skipped breakfast, or when Alex kept her distance in Madame Preston's class. Alex had a habit of giving herself breathing space whenever she felt offended by a friend. Leah knew she had hurt Alex because she wasn't convinced about the seriousness of Alex's feelings for Andrei—or about Andrei's feelings for her best friend. Leah hadn't changed her mind on that score, but after a good night's sleep she woke up thinking maybe she had spoken too soon. At the very least, she could have been gentler and a little more sensitive. But Alex was annoyed with her, and Leah knew she would have to live with that until Alex saw fit to break the ice. Leah herself preferred to get things out in the open and discuss them instantly. Clearing the air prevented bad vibes from festering, causing a small misunderstanding to become a major feud. But she had learned to respect Alex's ways, and she figured she'd have plenty of time to smooth things out between them at lunch.

Except Alex wasn't anywhere in sight at lunch, either. Leah scoured the Academy grounds for her friend. She searched the school's small cafeteria, the gazebo that graced the back lawn, and the redwood deck that extended from the art studio. Alex wasn't in any of the usual lunchtime haunts, leaving Leah alone and mystified. Alex couldn't be *that* upset. Unless Alex had realized Andrei wasn't in love with her, and was off somewhere nursing her wounds. Leah was going to feel pretty awkward around Alex if her hunch about Andrei's feelings was correct.

Leah left the greenhouse at the last possible moment, and as soon as she entered the Red Studio she knew she was wrong. Alex definitely did not look like a girl with a broken heart. Her cheeks were flushed pink and her eyes were bright as she stood, one leg up on the barre, doing stretches. The reason for Alex's exuberance was instantly clear. Andrei Levintoff had his hand on the well-pointed foot of her upraised leg. He corrected the positioning of her right shoulder, and Alex subtly shifted beneath his touch.

Leah's first glimpse of Andrei in practice clothes took her breath away. He wore a snug royal blue tank top and black tights. His gray leg warmers were bunched up around his ankles. Sunlight poured in through the open studio window, turning Andrei's sandy hair almost blond. He took a step back from Alex and eyed her critically. As he watched her stretch her torso forward over her upraised leg, he absently fingered the edge of the towel draped across his shoulders. He was lean, with a powerful compact build. The muscles in his legs were strongly defined and resembled coiled springs. His elevation, she thought, must be incredible.

"What's Andrei doing here?" Leah murmured. She was conscious of the highly charged atmosphere in the room. Andrei's presence was obviously causing a stir—the other girls seemed overly intent on their warm-ups.

"He's teaching," Linda Howe replied from the barre, eyeing herself critically in the mirror. With a tilt of her head and a subtle lengthening of her extended arm, she corrected the line of her arabesque.

"He's teaching repertory class?" Leah cried, astounded. Why hadn't she heard about this before? She looked around for Kay, angry that Kay hadn't told her the night before when she got back from her weekend. Obviously some announcement had been made on Saturday or Sunday. The upcoming coaching sessions with Andrei Levintoff were really big news at SFBA. Kay, being the irrepressible gossip that she was, should have told Leah the minute she had spotted her on the stairs. But romance, not dance, had been on Kay's mind just then. If Leah had known about Andrei, she would have prepared herself for class more carefully.

When she finally spotted Kay, her frown deepened. Kay had tied a scarlet ribbon around her bun and was wearing a red leotard that Leah hadn't seen before. A price tag poked out of the scooped-neck back. Kay had come prepared for their handsome new teacher. Leah self-consciously studied her own practice clothes: Her pink tights had gotten streaked from something blue in the wash, and she was wearing a nondescript blue leotard she wore only when she had fallen behind in her hand wash. To make matters worse, it had a run up the back and a gaping hole under the arm. Leah was usually fastidious about her appearance, although the repertory teacher wasn't strict about the school's tough dress regulations.

When Kay saw Leah, she waved enthusiastically and bounded over to her side. Faced with Kay's smile, Leah couldn't stay angry for long. Leah returned her grin, but was curious about Kay's high spirits. Kay was bursting with excitement, even though learning the company's classical repertory was not Kay's favorite activity. Lately Kay had made no secret of that. Last week she had rebelled by adding her own little flourishes to the girl's solo from *The Bluebird Variation*. Of course, it was Kay's newly discovered flair at making things up that had made her the star of Johnny Cullum's late-afternoon choreography workshop. Obviously, Andrei was the cause of Kay's change of heart about learning the classics. Leah had to admit, if she had known ahead of time about Andrei, she would have been pretty excited, too. This was one class she never would have risked being late for!

"Kay Larkin, why didn't you tell me?" Leah murmured under her breath, casting a quick glance in Andrei's direction.

"Really, Leah, you know how Andrei feels about Alex."

Leah looked up at the ceiling and groaned. "That's not what I meant. Why is Andrei Levintoff teaching this class? How come you didn't tell me last night? Look at how I'm dressed!" Leah said, fingering the worn fabric of her leotard.

Kay brushed off Leah's comment. "You look fine." She paused and regarded Leah shrewdly. "Besides, what's it to you?"

"Or to you?" Leah retorted instantly, indicating the high-cut leg of Kay's decidedly sexy outfit.

"Touché!" Kay shrugged good naturedly, then sighed. "Even if he *is* taken with Alex, it is nice to imagine that he might actually look at any one of us as more than just a dancer."

Kay's remark didn't sit right with Leah. "I don't see Alex's name tag on him, at least not yet," she commented, then wondered why the idea of Andrei's preference for Alex should bother her.

"Ha!" Kay exclaimed with great significance.

"Don't tell Alex that. She just spent her whole lunch hour at Jiminy Pizza with our new teacher." Kay's arch tone gave way to a wicked chuckle. "She's going to feel like a piece of lead trying to dance after that. Especially since Alex is usually so careful with her diet." Kay ruefully patted her own fairly flat stomach. She was trim, but because of her height and small build, she had trouble keeping her weight down. Discipline was not one of her strong points.

Leah digested Kay's information slowly. So that's why she'd been unable to find Alex at lunch. She wasn't avoiding Leah at all, and she certainly wasn't suffering alone over a broken heart. Leah felt a little foolish. While she was worrying about her friend, Alex had been out having a wonderful time, bending one of the least enforced of SFBA rules. Students were not supposed to leave the grounds during school hours, though an eye was closed at lunch, when the girls and boys often dashed across the street to break their diets at a fast-food stand.

Just then Andrei affectionately patted Alex's bottom. As Kay dissolved into a high-pitched giggle, Andrei turned and strode to the front of the room. The room fell silent even before he clapped his hands. Robert, the accompanist, adjusted the height of the piano bench, then rested his fingers on the keyboard, waiting for Andrei to begin.

"To the barre, girls. We warm up for fifteen minutes before class. I think you like it, no?" The girls scampered to the wooden barres that lined three walls of the studio.

Leah hurried to a position across the way from Alex. Alex hadn't acknowledged her presence, so

Leah had no way of knowing if her friend was actually upset with her, but she instinctively knew to give Alex space, at least until class was over. She'd get a chance later to talk to Alex about whatever misunderstanding had occurred the night before.

Andrei's barre work, as he promised, was short. Leah was impressed with his combinations of the exercises. As she toweled off the perspiration from her face and neck, she couldn't remember any class she'd taken where a quarter of an hour at the barre had left her so thoroughly warmed up, and so completely tired.

She stood with one hand on her hip and tucked the wisps of her blond hair back into her bun. As she listened to Andrei and watched him demonstrate the entrance of the corps de ballet in the second act of *La Bayadère*, she forgot all about how ragged she looked, Alex's budding romance, and how deeply her muscles ached after her weekend break from dance.

Andrei's approach to dance was different from anything Leah had experienced so far in her short ballet career. He was, after all, a product of one of the most famous schools in the world, the Vaganova Institute, the official school of the Kirov. Ever since seeing tapes of the Kirov's version of *The Sleeping Beauty* and *Swan Lake*, Leah had longed to study in Russia someday. But for an American girl that was an impossible dream. This afternoon Leah eagerly absorbed every nuance of Andrei's demonstration.

The entrance of the corps de ballet that Andrei was having them dance was one of the most famous and difficult pieces of ensemble work in the entire classical repertory. The long sequence of arabesque penchées followed by deep back bends required precision on the part of each girl. As the line of dancers made its way across the stage in a slow procession, Leah realized the ballet demanded great individual strength and a unified company style. All the girls in the class were capable of doing the steps, but very few gave the impression of really dancing them. And they hadn't danced together or studied under the same teacher long enough to perform as a real corps. Leah knew a new production of the ballet was going to be part of the company's repertory during the winter season. The students were spending a lot of time learning it, though it would be a couple of years before any of them had an opportunity to dance it.

Andrei motioned the girls to the back of the room and indicated that Alex was to be first in line.

"First we listen to the music." Motioning to the accompanist, he closed his eyes and with his hands marked out the choreography for the girls. After a moment of absorbing the soft strains of the sensuous music, he began to speak. "You hear that this music is like what you hear when you sleep. Like—" he fished for the word "—like from a dream. This scene may be just someone's dream. You must move as if you are not quite real women anymore, but only the sad ghosts of women who once loved."

In spite of his broken English Leah completely understood what he meant. Now if only her body could carry out his instructions. She leaned forward from her spot and watched as he demonstrated the steps, talking all the while. Leah couldn't believe the way his body gave way to the music and the choreography. He was more graceful than any girl in the room.

"Now," he said, not missing a beat of the music. "The first girl steps out of the wings. The stage is all dark. Imagine it is a night but no big moon in the sky. Only light is on the first girl wearing white. Do not forget the cloth...." He looked up and cast a quick questioning glance at Alex and mumbled something in Russian and motioned from his wrist up to where the sleeve of the girl's costume would be.

"Chiffon!" She supplied the word.

"That is it—chiffon. Imagine the chiffon and move like the moon shining through it."

Leah caught her breath at the image, but forced herself to pay close attention as he continued moving, not missing a beat. "Two very important things you remember, no? When you make like this"—he demonstrated a deep penché, leaning over his bent supporting leg until his raised leg was stretched in a long, high arabesque—"you must be well over your hip and pulled up. You do not sit over bent leg. You pull up even more when you plié — like this." Then he took two steps forward and leaned into the deep arch of his back. "You catch the back here." He straightened up and stopped demonstrating, then pulled Alex toward him, and tapped her back just under the shoulder blades. "Do not make the back fall down like a badly built wall of children's blocks. Arch it, making it long, not short. All the little bones of the spine are connected with material that bends. Think of that." He motioned for Robert to start the music. As he took the two steps forward, he reminded the girls, "You are ghosts of beautiful princesses, you must remember to be mysterious. But you are still in love, no?"

Leah wasn't the only girl who gasped aloud as he cast an unmistakably warm glance toward Alex. Now Leah was sure Alex was right in assuming that Andrei was attracted to her. No guy looked at a girl like that unless he had more than friendship on his mind. Despair washed over Leah. First Chrissy, now Alex. She wondered if anyone would ever look at her that way.

After he demonstrated the combination of steps and penchées for several more bars, he lined the girls up behind Alex and asked them to begin.

Leah stood in line watching Alex carefully, envying the girl's Russian training. The steps seemed to be made for her supple back and high extension. Even in a black leotard, Alex moved as if she were wearing a fluffy white tutu with chiffon veils attached to her arms. The girls following Alex had a more difficult time. Linda got the penché right, but her back wasn't quite flexible enough. Kay bravely struggled to look mysterious and elegant, but the steps didn't suit her natural staccato quality of movement at all. Pamela Hunter was the last to go before Leah. Trying to picture herself entering from the wings of a big stage, Leah prepared herself to begin. As she watched Pamela take her first steps forward, Leah was impressed. Somehow Pamela, though giving an impression of strength and one of liquid movement, looked better than anyone so far except Alex. Apparently Andrei thought so, too.

"You with the red hair. Very good. Perfect."

Then it was Leah's turn. She realized Andrei's eyes were on her. She counted the music inwardly and winced when she wobbled on her penché and Andrei shouted a correction about pulling her weight up over her hip. The second go-round she managed a bit better, but by then Andrei was calling out instructions to the girl behind her.

After class was over, Leah made sure she left the dressing room with Alex.

"Hey, stranger," she called after her friend, as the tall, dark-haired girl headed down the hall. Alex turned around and waited for Leah to catch up. Leah couldn't quite read her expression. At least Alex didn't look angry. "Why do I get the impression you are trying to avoid me?" Leah tried to sound light but fidgeted with the strap of her bag, waiting for Alex to answer.

"I am not trying to avoid you," Alex said, as they started down the stairs.

Leah exhaled slowly. "You could have fooled me," she said. "You weren't around at breakfast, or at lunch, and you didn't save a place for me at the barre this morning."

Alex laughed. "I'm sorry about that. But it was probably good for you to work on the other side of the room for a change. You know what Madame says about it being better to alternate what side of the body you exercise first. Starting on the left is my bad habit. You shouldn't do what I do, Leah. You may learn some wrong things."

"I think you just forgot all about me," Leah teased, opening the French doors that led to SFBA's sprawling backyard. As they proceeded toward the art studio, Leah's tone grew more serious.

"Actually, Alex, I thought you were upset because of last night. Tell me the truth—weren't you a little angry with me?"

Alex looked Leah in the eye and hesitated, "Yes," she admitted reluctantly. "This morning at breakfast I was, but then—"

Leah cut her off firmly. "Well, you should have been. I was a little rough on you about Andrei, and from what I can see, I may have been wrong."

Alex's expression softened into a smile. "Thanks for that, Leah. I did feel you were being unfair last night. You do not know Andrei the way I do. He does not act like a friend toward me anymore. It is more than that." She pulled Leah's hand through her arm and looked around. Seeing they were alone, she continued in a low, confidential voice. "You see, I met him for breakfast and then lunch. We seem to have so much to talk about."

Suddenly everything became clear to Leah. "And you can speak Russian together." Leah couldn't help but think how awful it must be to speak a different language from everyone else. She knew Alex was exceptionally gifted at languages, but even for Alex it must be strange never to be able to express what she really thought.

Alex paused and regarded Leah in silence. After a moment she said slowly, "Yes. I had not thought about it like that. But it makes me feel more at home being with him." A wistful note entered her voice. She looked away from Leah, but her soft words were clearly audible. "I did not realize how homesick I was until he arrived."

"Imagine how he feels," Leah added. "He hasn't even got family here like you do."

"I know. He worries about what is happening to

his family. And I think he will miss Russia more than I do. I have lived here since I was young. He's almost twenty." The girls were silent for a moment, but then Alex laughed a secret sort of laugh. "That is why this is all so special."

She turned to Leah, and her expressive eyes were shining. "I have never felt this way before about a man. I do not feel like eating, and I cannot sleep at night. When he is away from me, I cannot stand it. I know he feels the same. I can tell." Alex stopped talking and turned to Leah with a blissful expression on her face. "I know this is love, Leah."

Leah sensed the conversation was heading in a dangerous direction. She had seen some evidence today that Andrei seemed to regard Alex as more than a friend. But love? To Leah that was a very special word, and Andrei had only been in town a couple of days. Did love grow that fast? Leah knew Alex wanted her to agree. Leah was Alex's closest friend at the school, the one whose opinion Alex really respected. Leah weighed her words carefully before she spoke. "I don't know anything about love myself—not yet," she admitted honestly. "I don't know if I'd recognize it if it hit me in the face and had a great big label on it. But I could see today I was wrong. He's more than a friend to you." Leah felt safe saying that.

But for Alex it obviously wasn't enough. She kicked some loose gravel off the walk and studied her feet. When she spoke again, she pointedly changed the subject. "So tonight is the big night."

Leah decided to play along for now. "You mean the Alvarezes' party. I didn't really understand

Madame's announcement about it last week at assembly."

"Every year we have a couple of these get-togethers. It's not really for us. In fact, SFBA students, as well as the company members, are more or less on display. We have to act like proper young dancers." Alex's look of disdain made Leah laugh. "Corporate and individual contributors attend."

Leah looked surprised. "How big is the Alvarezes' house?"

Alex laughed. "Very big, but not that big. Only the most important contributors come to the parties. We have galas and performances at the Opera House for the rest of them." Alex stopped and squinted. Leah followed her glance. She spotted Andrei far across the lawn. His powerful stride was unmistakable. He was in the middle of a group of boys heading out the front gate. A dreamy sigh escaped Alex's lips. Then she caught Leah watching her and turned away.

"So what are you going to wear tonight?" she said offhandedly.

Leah tried to get her mind off of Alex's predicament. If Alex was right about Andrei, then good for her. If she was wrong, Leah didn't want to be in the position of saying "I told you so." She'd rather play the role of good friend, a warm and comfortable shoulder to cry on.

Chapter 4

"And this young lady," said Madame Preston, placing a firm hand on Leah's shoulder and turning her to face the party's hostess, "is Leah Stephenson. She's our latest Golden Gate scholarship winner."

Mrs. Alvarez's dark, sparkling eyes surveyed Leah. "Welcome to SFBA—I know my welcome's a bit late," the small woman said with a charming little laugh. "But sometimes we don't get to meet the new students for several months."

"I'm pleased to meet you," Leah said a bit stiffly, offering her hand. To her surprise, Mrs. Alvarez didn't shake it, but took it between both of hers and gave it a warm, companionable squeeze. Instantly Leah decided she liked this woman and hoped she'd have a chance to get to know the company's chief benefactor under less strained circumstances.

For Leah, at least, the semiannual party for the major sponsors of the Bay Area Ballet and its school was very strained indeed. She had never liked big parties, even with kids she knew back home in San Lorenzo in junior high school. She felt comfortable with people individually, or if she were performing before an audience. Dancing in front of hundreds was somehow easier than making conversation in a room full of elegantly dressed strangers. The fact that Madame had singled her out to meet some of the most important people in the room made Leah proud but nervous. She felt as if she were expected to say something clever, not just stand and grin and blush like a silly fifteen-year-old at her first party. Leah wasn't good at just saying things, making small talk with people who weren't dancers.

To make matters worse, Leah had more on her mind tonight than the party. For the first time since James's accident at a high school dance demonstration, Leah had to confront Diana Chen. The company was back from its European tour. Tonight was the first time company members had had a chance to mingle with SFBA students. Diana was the company's top young ballerina, a very gifted yet very competitive dancer who was sometimes Leah's teacher. Diana had had her sights set on the talented James as the perfect partner to catapult her into the national limelight. Somehow Diana blamed Leah for his injury, since Leah, at his request, had failed to report it. Now that James had left the school and was headed to New York to begin his professional career with the Joffrey Ballet, Leah was afraid Diana's wrath was going to make life at SFBA very difficult for her. So far, Leah had found it easy to avoid Diana, who was very visible in a flaming-red strapless dress, but the party wasn't that big.

Before Leah could continue to worry about it,

Mrs. Alvarez had put her arm around her, and with her other hand beckoned for a server. "Would you like some fruit punch?" she asked Leah. Then turning toward Madame, she said, "I'll introduce Leah around. It will give me a chance to get to know her."

Leah cast a shy, almost desperate glance over her shoulder at Madame. The school director waved her away with a smile on her stern, angular face. Leah took a deep breath. The look in Madame's piercing gray eyes had told Leah all she needed to know. She was one of Madame's star pupils, and it was up to her, Leah Kimberly Stephenson, to act the part. She swallowed hard and racked her brains for something to say to Mrs. Alvarez.

Fortunately Mrs. Alvarez was an old hand at parties and introductions. She regaled Leah with a constant stream of pleasantries that required absolutely no answer but a smile. All the while, the smartly dressed dark-haired woman steered her from one little knot of people to the next, introducing her with a flash of her bejeweled hands and somehow doing it so Leah's job became quite easy. She just had to smile, say yes or no, or very occasionally repeat her name and mention Miss Greene, her former teacher back in San Lorenzo who ran Hannah Greene's School of Dance and Theater Arts.

Just as Leah began to think that her increasingly stiff smile would be permanently etched on her face, she was rescued by Alex and Andrei, who walked over, hand in hand. Alex was dressed in a simple slim black dress and wore gold-hoop earrings; a black velvet bow was pinned to her dark hair, which was fastened in a tight bun. Andrei wore an elegant suit that Leah thought became him perfectly. He greeted Leah with his usual warm smile, but in a moment Mrs. Alvarez had claimed him. Leah was grateful for a chance to escape the spotlight.

"Oh, Alex, I don't think I can take another one of these parties," she wailed quietly, dying for a breath of fresh air.

"You'll get used to them," she said, her eyes following Andrei's progress through the crowd. "They usually are more fun than this one. Sometimes there is a live rock band and lots of dancing."

Leah cast a suspicious glance around the elegantly furnished house. Somehow bands, musicians, and lots of dancing didn't seem to fit in with the tastefully quiet decor.

Alex watched her expression carefully, and gave her a little shake. "Not here," Alex chided with a throaty laugh. "Never at one of the benefactor's houses. They are all too old." She dropped her voice to a discreet whisper and steered Leah into a less crowded area of the room. "Most fundraising events are the big galas or special student performances. Afterward, there are very big parties with ten times as many people. They're more fun because you don't have to talk to everyone," she said, making a face.

Kay was waving at both of them from across the room. "What do you think Kay wants?" Leah said, giving Alex a nudge.

"She found out some juicy bit of news, I guess," Alex said. "Let's go over and find out."

"You go ahead," Leah told her. "I'll join you in

a little while. Where's the bathroom? I feel like my hair is about to come down."

Alex pointed Leah in the right direction, then went over to talk to Kay. To avoid the press of people, Leah detoured through the mahogany-paneled den, where the crowd was definitely thinner. The bookshelves reached up to the ceiling and the yellow-shaded lamps cast a warm glow over the room. Leah was tempted to linger there, but she spotted Diana Chen in a corner. Her back was toward Leah, and she was talking animatedly to a corporate contributor Leah had just met, but whose name she couldn't remember. Leah kept close to the wall and breathed a sign of relief when she reached the hall undetected. It was a bit cooler there and Leah quickly saw why. Two opened louvered doors led out to the terrace. Leah felt a sudden impulse to get out of the stuffy, noisy house into the quiet dark of evening. Before she got a chance, a hand touched her shoulder, causing Leah to jump.

"Sorry. I didn't mean to scare you," Diana Chen said. She took her hand away to flick her long ponytail over her shoulder. Leah couldn't believe how incredibly beautiful the young ballerina looked. Her straight black hair had the luster of satin, and came halfway down to her waist.

But Diana's beauty didn't erase all the terrible things she had said to Leah. Leah wouldn't allow herself to be rude, but she didn't have to be friendly, either. "Oh, hello," she said with a coolness of which she didn't think herself capable.

Diana arched one perfectly shaped eyebrow. Leah watched with surprise as Diana made an obvious effort to remain as composed as possible. "Listen, Leah, I know what happened between us before the company tour was far from pleasant. While I was away, I thought a lot about you and James. I wanted to tell you I'm sorry, truly sorry, for whatever I said to you then. I was angry, and ..." Diana seemed to find the next words hard, but Leah sensed her determination to voice her feelings. "I was afraid. For James, and for myself. Not—" she added quickly, "that that excuses anything I've done."

Leah was amazed. "Are you apologizing to me?"

A smile began to form at the corners of Diana's perfectly painted red lips. "Yes."

"I—I don't know what to say," Leah replied, leaning back against the intricate woodwork of the wainscoting. "Thank you, I guess." She didn't quite trust Diana, and wasn't sure why.

Diana seemed to realize that. "I know I said some very hard things, Leah. But this isn't the place to talk about it. Maybe, once I get back on schedule, we could go to lunch and talk then. I would like to be friends," Diana added, and a look of real warmth came into her eyes.

Leah couldn't help but respond to Diana's apparent sincerity. "I'd like that very much, Diana, I really would."

"Then it's a date," Diana said, looking genuinely excited. "We'll make it definite sometime next week. Things are a bit crazy right now, these first few days back from the tour and all."

Leah was about to ask her about the tour when a young man she'd never seen before burst into the hall and hurried toward Diana's side. "Di, you won't believe who's here." A moment later he was pulling Diana after him through the crowd. Before she disappeared, she waved helplessly at Leah as the young man led her away.

Leah flashed her a thumbs up sign, then took advantage of the deserted hall to step out through the open doors into the night. She trailed her hand along the railing that ran the length of the veranda. Music and the buzz of party conversation floated out from the brightly lit Spanish-style ranch house. Leah rubbed her bare arms in the cool breeze, shivering slightly through the silky fabric of her party dress. It was a cold night, but the stars seemed close enough to touch in the clear inland sky. Leah forced herself to forget the chilly weather. She feasted her eyes on the expanse of corrals and stables and the shadowy shapes of vineyards beyond the lamplit driveways and outbuildings of the ranch proper. Horses huddled in a near corner of the corral, and an occasional stomp of a hoof, or a whinny, drifted across the dry yard toward Leah.

Leah's mind wandered back to her encounter in the hallway with Diana. It seemed too good to be true that the proud young ballerina had actually apologized to Leah. But then, perhaps Leah had been too hard on Diana these past few weeks, thinking of her as some kind of rival or enemy. Not that Leah had been the first one to bring that up. Diana had decided Leah was competition and then had made life quite miserable for her when she was learning the *Romeo and Juliet* pas de deux with James.

Still, Leah reflected, she might have felt the same way in Diana's position. Maybe it was the wide open space of the Alvarez ranch and the crystal-clear air that influenced her, but standing

there in the dark alone on the veranda, Leah
made a firm decision to give Diana the benefit of
the doubt. She'd try to keep an open mind while
having lunch with her. She'd rather have Diana
Chen on her side rooting for her than against her.
Besides, Diana was a wonderful dancer, and Leah
was well aware that she could learn a lot just
from being around her.

Behind her a man cleared his throat.

Leah turned around, startled. The guilty ex-
pres-sion on her face quickly gave way to a puzzled smile. "Ardrei?" she asked, not quite able to
make out the shadowy figure as he stood with his
back to the house lights.

"Yes, Leah, it is I."

He joined her at the railing, peering down at
her. He didn't say anything, but she could read
the expression on his face. Without words he was
asking her if it was all right for him to be there.

Leah smiled tentatively. "It's a little cold out
here."

Andrei instantly took off his jacket. Leah wanted
to die of embarrassment. "I hadn't meant it as a
hint," she gasped. "I don't mind being cold, I
mean—I'm not that cold." The more she said the
sillier she sounded. Andrei disregarded her dis-
may and draped his jacket over her half-bare
shoulders. It was warm, and Leah found herself
grateful for it.

"Th—thank you," she stammered.

"It is okay," he said. "You have a very pretty
dress. I like it. . . ." He hesitated, and Leah silently thanked her mom, who had convinced her
that her new purple miniskirt was not the right
thing for a fund-raising party and had dragged

her to the mall while she was home for the weekend to buy her something "decent" to wear. "But," Andrei went on, "it does not protect you from the wind."

"But you'll be cold now," Leah protested feebly. Andrei's stilted sentences sounded like poetry when he spoke, because of his wonderful accent.

"Not at all. I like cold air. Inside there are too many people—it is hot and hard to breathe."

Leah agreed wholeheartedly, but she was surprised Andrei minded the crowd. He seemed so urbane and sophisticated while he socialized with all the influential people at the party. He never seemed to be at a loss for words and hadn't looked the least bit uncomfortable. And as far as she knew, he hadn't even met most of the company members until tonight, but he was very much at ease with them.

"These people, they are very rich," Andrei stated suddenly, leaning his elbows on the railing and peering out into the night.

Leah was suddenly conscious of the great gulf between them. Something in Andrei's tone made her wary of how she answered. Though she would have assumed Mrs. Alvarez to be a snob, she had turned out to be anything but. Leah didn't want Andrei to get the wrong impression of wealthy Americans.

She reached back in her mind for something she had learned recently in her social studies class. Mrs. Gilette had been talking about how California's geography had influenced the course of its history and, finally, its economic growth. She discussed the vineyards as an example. Leah turned toward Andrei and tried to convey to him as clearly as she could what she remembered. "Mr. and Mrs. Alvarez's parents, and probably grandparents, planted grapevines here. They didn't have much money at first, but as the American wine business grew, they became very successful."

Andrei nodded, and a sigh escaped his lips. "It is good, no, to see a farm doing so well?"

His comment surprised her. "Why, yes." Leah paused and frowned in the dark. "I never thought of a winery as a farm before." Suddenly, she saw Andrei in a new light. "You sound like you know about farms," she commented, surprise evident in her voice.

He laughed, but somehow his laugh had a melancholy note to it. Leah realized all at once that he was lonely. Not much older than herself, Andrei was homesick. And because of his decision to defect, he'd never see his native land again. She wondered suddenly about his family. What had happened to them? To his friends back in Leningrad? How would she feel if she could never see her own mother, or Kay, or Alex? Leah longed to ask him about these things, but some instinct prompted her not to. Maybe she would someday when he had been here longer, when he was more used to her. Leah felt a blush color her cheek. What in the world was she thinking of? Andrei Levintoff was on the verge of a brilliant international career. After the Bay Area Ballet's winter season was over, she'd probably never see him again. She bit her tongue and watched him out of the corner of her eye. She was glad that the lights on the veranda were dim. At least he couldn't see how embarrassed she was.

Andrei didn't say anything more for a while, then slowly turned to face the house. Hoisting himself onto the railing, he straddled it and faced Leah. "I should know about farms. If as a child I did not have this gift to dance, I would be a person who farms."

"A farmer," Leah mechanically corrected him.

"Yes, a farmer," Andrei repeated, obviously eager to improve his English. "I was born on a farm—we call them collectives—in the Ukraine. The farms there are very big and have the richest earth in the Soviet Union. My family also has a small piece of land behind the house. What we grow there we sell ourselves. But farmers do not become rich there, and my father wanted me and my sister to have a better life. My sister becomes a scientist at university and I dance."

Leah stared at him, and suddenly everything made sense: the way he seemed comfortable outdoors.

"I'm sort of from a farm, too," Leah said, for the first time not ashamed to admit it. Everyone at SFBA tended to make fun of her small-town background.

"You are?" Andrei swung his leg back over the rail and jumped down. He faced Leah with a happy smile on his face, dispelling his sad mood of the last few minutes. "I knew there was something different about you. None of the other girls I met here are quite like you. I feel as if I have always known you, though you are an American girl and I am Russian." He stood before her, just grinning at her, with his hands in the pockets of his well-tailored gray slacks. Just when the silence might have grown awkward between them, he asked, "What part of America are you from?"

For a moment Leah was surprised at the question. Everyone took one look at her, listened to her accent, and knew she was a native-born Californian. Then she remembered Andrei was new to the country. "I'm from here."

Andrei looked back out over the sprawling ranch, then back to her.

Leah giggled, beginning to feel more at ease with the great dancer. "No, not *here* exactly. Certainly not Sonoma County, but farther south in California. Not far from Salinas," she added, thinking of the biggest town anywhere near San Lorenzo.

"What kind of farm did you live on?" Andrei asked, and before she could explain about her home, he made another, more urgent inquiry. "And how do you feel about living in the city away from your farm?"

A month ago Leah would have told him she hated San Francisco, in spite of the endless excitement, but just the night before, she had realized it was her real home now and that she had grown to love it. "I like living at Mrs. Hanson's," she said, wanting to explain why. "It's different from my home town, San Lorenzo." Leah fell silent trying to find the right words. Why, she wondered inwardly, were words so hard to come by when she was talking with Andrei? "Back home, my parents lived on what used to be a farm. It was cheap when they bought it, before I was born. They rented out some of the land to local farmers. Our town is famous for artichokes," she added. Andrei looked puzzled. Since she didn't have a Russian-English dictionary on hand, she explained to him it was a vegetable that had petals like a flower.

"When my father died—" she continued.

Andrei stopped smiling. "You no longer have your father?" He reached for Leah's hand and held it. "You are very young to lose a parent."

Leah just nodded. Tears misted her eyes, but she took a moment to catch her breath, and she managed not to cry. "Yes, I lost him when I was just nine." Before Andrei could react again, Leah hurried on. Thinking about her father still hurt, and it felt strange having Andrei hold her hand. With the excuse of fishing in her bag for a tissue, Leah gently pulled her hand away and kept talking. "My mother sold a lot of our land after he died to the people on the farm next door, and now she runs a really great business. She's a computer programmer and systems consultant for farmers."

Leah could feel Andrei's eyes on her in the dark. When he didn't comment on her mother's job, she decided to change the subject. Besides, she was curious about his background. "Do you miss your farm?"

"All the time," he said, more vehemently than she'd expected. He looked across the grounds, outward into the dark night. "Sometimes you can reach your finger up to the stars and pretend to touch them."

"Like tonight," Leah half whispered, warmed by the fact that Andrei shared her feelings.

"Yes, like this," he said, turning around and taking her hand again. But when he spoke, his voice had a faraway ring to it. "I never liked Leningrad. All big cities are the same—the bright lights and all the people always going so fast. In Russia people do not go as fast as here, even in the cities, but still, at the farm it was so quiet, you could almost hear the earth breathe."

"Then why did you leave?" Leah asked, puzzled. She had never met a dancer who would have preferred to live a peaceful, rural life before. Most dancers were born show people, in love with makeup, bright stage lights, and above all, the audiences who came to watch them.

Andrei looked at her as if he didn't quite believe her question. "Because this gift I have is my chance to have a better life. I love to dance, and a friend in New York tells me I can someday have a place in the country and still dance if I live here in America. I would like that dream to come true."

Impulsively Leah squeezed his hand. "Well, in America if you want a dream to come true, you wish upon a star. I wanted more than anything in the world to be a dancer when I was little. Every night I would wish on a special star, and my wish is coming true."

Andrei laughed, and his laugh didn't sound sad anymore. "We do that in Russia, too—when we are children. I almost forgot about that. Do you think it works for people who are not children anymore?" His twinkling blue eyes sought Leah's. She suddenly felt a strong bond between them.

"We have a saying here—it can't hurt you to try."

"Then I try."

Leah watched him look up and study the sky. Then he closed his eyes and his lips began to move slightly, but she couldn't hear what he said.

She was still looking at him when he opened his eyes.

"Did I do it right?" he asked seriously.

"Perfect!" Leah answered with equal solemnity.

Then Andrei reached over and planted a friendly kiss on Leah's cheek and squeezed her in his strong arms. "One wish I had when I come here to this city is already true. I have found new friends."

"I would like to be your friend," Leah said earnestly, and her hand couldn't help but touch the place Andrei had just kissed. Her heart was thumping faster than usual, and Leah felt happier than she had in months.

A commotion inside the house broke the spell of their intimate moment.

"What's happening?" Leah wondered.

"We go see, no?" Andrei hooked her hand through his arm and energetically strode toward the French doors, pushing them open.

Leah winced, horrified to find herself face-to-face with Pamela Hunter. Pam's green eyes darted from Leah to Andrei, then lingered on Leah's hand, the one holding Andrei's arm. Leah fought back the impulse to pull her hand away. Being close to Andrei like this meant nothing, so there was nothing to be embarrassed about. Let Pam draw whatever conclusions she wished. As Andrei had said, they were friends, just friends, Leah repeated inwardly, wishing her cheeks weren't so hot.

"I was wondering if you two had evaporated," Pam drawled with a flutter of her thick dark lashes. "Alex ..." She drew out the name ever so slightly, and the faint smile on her pouty lips didn't fool

Leah one bit. Pam was about to cause trouble. Her body stiffened as Pam continued in a soft, purring voice, " ... has been looking for Andrei for hours now, absolute hours! She'll be glad to hear you didn't desert her, and were just out on the terrace taking the air." Pam gently rapped Andrei's arm with her long, slender fingers. Her brilliant pink nails seemed to startle Andrei.

He stared at her hands, then at her face as if trying to place her. Pam's miniskirt was shot through with copper threads that brought out the red in her hair. With her hair down, dangling earrings, and tastefully applied yet heavy makeup, she barely resembled the girl Andrei had complimented in class that day. Leah took the opportunity to step away from Andrei, shoving her hands into the pockets of her dress. Standing so close to him had been perfectly innocent, just like his kiss. But Leah had a feeling that Pam was going to make sure the version Alex heard of Leah's interlude on the veranda didn't sound very innocent at all. Leah chided herself inwardly and followed Pam and Andrei into the crowded living room. Now Alex would think Leah was trying to steal Andrei from her. Why, even the night before in the boardinghouse kitchen, she had seemed a bit jealous of Leah, and now, whatever Pam said would just fuel the fire. Leah couldn't resist wrinkling her nose at Pam behind her back.

Pamela Hunter was an ongoing problem at SFBA. The two girls had met in September when they arrived in San Francisco for the Academy entrance auditions. At first Leah had been drawn to the vivacious redhead from Atlanta. She knew so much about dance—and everything else. Alongside of her Leah felt every inch the naive, small-town girl she was. Pam had danced in regional productions of *The Nutcracker* back home in Goergia; she had a brilliantly athletic technique and a powerful jump that Leah admired and envied. Unfortunately, Pam proved to have an equally powerful competitive sense. Nothing and no one would get in Pam Hunter's way en route to the top. Leah hadn't even realized there was a top, at least as far as SFBA was concerned. She had enough to keep her busy proving herself worthy of the prestigious school during entrance-week exams. Pam had her heart set on being the best, the most memorable dancer at the Academy. It was only a matter of time before she had zeroed in on Leah as being her only real competition and tried to sabotage her audition behind her back. By substituting Leah's audition piece for her own, she tried to steal Leah's thunder.

But in spite of Pam's tactics Leah emerged as the first girl in two years to receive the coveted Golden Gate Award, given only occasionally to an entering dancer of unusual promise. From that moment on Pam had hated Leah with a passion. After several months of Pam's backbiting and cutting remarks, Leah figured she'd better get used to it. But as Madame Preston rapped her hand on the top of a table to get the crowd's attention, Leah had a feeling she was in for a new round of troubles with Pam.

The gray-haired director looked around the room until the individual conversations diminished into silence. With a gesture so familiar to Leah, she smoothed the slim skirt of her pale silk suit and then smiled.

"I am pleased to announce that the Saturday after next we will have a special student matinee." A murmur of enthusiasm rippled through the crowd. "The performance, as I'm sure some of you may have guessed, is to be held for an exclusive audience of major individual and corporate sponsors of the company and the school. It will be held at the Opera House."

Leah and several other new students gasped aloud. To dance at the Opera House so soon! Leah couldn't wait to write home about this stroke of luck.

Madame went on. "This year our Student Matinee will have a new look to it. First of all, we will do the entire second act of *La Bayadère*." A gasp went up from the assembled SFBA students. "Next, we've decided it would be challenging and fun to have a program of mostly contemporary work, some already in the company repertory, and some pieces newly choreographed for the occasion."

A ripple of excitement went through the room as Madame continued.

"To help spark interest in this performance and, of course, sell tickets," the former ballerina said delightedly, "the Bay Area Ballet's distinguished guest, Andrei Levintoff, has generously offered to make his West Coast debut in our school Matinee and will partner a student of his choosing in a pas de deux he will choreograph himself."

Applause and cheers rang out in the room. Leah clapped her hands over her mouth and almost screamed aloud. Frantically she sought the crowd for Alex—what great luck for her friend! Andrei would be sure to pick her. She was a senior student, probably the best in the school right now, and Andrei so obviously liked her. Leah couldn't spot Alex, but vowed that the moment Madame stopped speaking, she'd find her and offer her congratulations.

Leah turned her attentions back to Madame. She had missed a little, but it only took a moment to figure out that she was talking about Johnny Cullum's choreography class.

"... and one original student work will be selected and performed. So, as you see, it will be a very full program, bound to draw a large and appreciative audience." For a moment Madame dropped her guard and smiled the warm, encouraging smile that her students did not see very often. She warned them affectionately, "The next two weeks are going to be pretty demanding, and I want you all to be in top form at class first thing in the morning."

Chapter 5

Dear Leah,

It was so nice to talk to you last night. For me, it was special to be with you where we could touch the stars. I would like to see you this afternoon at 4:00 P.M. in the west practice room on third floor.

Andrei Levintoff

The note was scrawled in Andrei's almost childlike block letters and continued after his signature. But before Leah could read the short postscript, Alex came flying through the front door of the school. Leah had imagined Alex had been off having breakfast with Andrei again until she had found the note pinned up on the bulletin board with rehearsal schedules and class announcements. Now Leah wondered if Andrei was seeing Alex after all—the note was *so* inti-mate. Feeling guilty, she stuffed the letter back into the envelope and found it hard to meet her friend's eyes.

"What a beautiful morning," Alexandra cried, elated, impulsively hugging Leah. Alex squinted at the board, her practical side taking over, and made a couple of notes before turning again to Leah. "Wasn't that a great party last night? Andrei told me he had a wonderful time."

Leah felt herself turn red. Her fingers gripped the envelope more tightly, wrinkling it. "Uh, nice— yes, it *was* nice." Leah felt very uncomfortable. Andrei had just left her a note, a personal note, about their being together the night before. Touching the stars—it was such a romantic thing to say! But Alex was her best friend, and in love with Andrei.

"And do you believe it, Andrei is actually going to dance with—" Alex cut herself off, but Leah suspected she was about to say "with me." Probably Andrei had already talked to her about it over breakfast. Alex collected herself quickly and finished her sentence. "With one of us."

"I think it's great, Alex. I really do," Leah said earnestly. Alex's having the opportunity to dance with Andrei made sense to her. Alex was a senior student, and with her Russian training, she would make a great partner for Andrei. It was Alex's off-stage relationship with Andrei that was bothering Leah. She didn't want Alex to get hurt because of her. Kicking her toe against the wall, she wondered exactly what to do.

The grandfather clock near the entranceway chimed nine times. "We're going to be late for Madame's class!" Alex warned. She started to hurry toward the stairs, then stopped to wait for Leah.

Strains of piano music floating down from the second floor meant class was about to start.

Leah thought fast. She didn't want to be with Alex just then. She needed time to think about Andrei's note, what he meant, and exactly what she would do about it. "I haven't really checked the schedule yet," Leah said, going through the motions of searching her bag for a pen. "Madame always says we should study the call-board thoroughly," Leah recited brightly. "I'll be up in a minute."

"Ciao!" said Alex, waving good-bye as she headed up the staircase to the second floor.

The moment Alex's footsteps died away, Leah pulled out the crumpled note. Leah reread the body of the letter quickly before scanning the postscript. Her heart sank. Andrei's parting words merely reminded her to wear her practice clothes. Leah read the whole thing before putting it away. Andrei's message had begun in a romantic vein, but now Leah could see all he really wanted was that she dance for him. It took a moment before the full meaning of it dawned on her. *Dance with him!* Leah's disappointment vanished as her spirits soared; she felt as if she were riding some kind of emotional roller coaster. If Andrei Levintoff wanted to meet her for some kind of private practice session, that could mean only one thing— he had chosen her over Alex to be his partner. Leah's fierce determination to become a great dancer made it easy to push everything else aside. Andrei might not be interested in her romantically, but his professional interest in her was a whole different ball game. Leah breathed a sigh of relief. Competing with Alex over a choice role was a situation that Leah was used to dealing with. Leah and Alex had been pitted against each other before, and their friendship had weathered the strain. When it came right down to it, she was glad not to have to worry about Andrei's feelings for her—competing with Alex over a guy made Leah feel like a cheat.

The clock struck a quarter past the hour. Leah carelessly stuffed the note into the depths of her bag and dashed up the stairs, taking them two at a time.

Later that afternoon Leah walked into the west practice room and bumped right into Alex. "What are you doing here?" The words popped out before Leah could stop herself.

"Same to you!" Alex retorted, then added in a brusque voice, "But I'm glad you are, in the long run." Leah barely had time to digest the fact that she was not going to be alone with Andrei at this rehearsal when Alex elbowed her in the side.

Leah was about to complain, then she saw why Alex was on edge. Pamela Hunter was strutting around the room, flinging open the windows.

"I hate stuffy places. I simply don't know how you can stand this studio. It's so unbearably oppressive, you can't breathe in here, let alone dance." Pam positioned herself at the barre and checked her reflection in the mirror. She must have been pleased with what she saw, because she smiled at herself, then squeezed her feet together in a very tight fifth position. Leah's knees ached just watching her force her turnout. Pam began a series of ronds de jambes à terre, the strongly arched foot of her working leg inscribing the floor with enviable precision. Somehow, she made the familiar exercise look very sexy.

"Does this mean what I think it means?" Leah asked suddenly, realizing what it meant that all of them were there.

Alex nodded. Her full lips were tightly pressed together as she put her hand on the nearest barre and began a series of battements. The kicks were high and fast, and Leah had the impression Alex was pretending to kick someone—and you didn't have to be Sherlock Holmes to figure out that a certain redhead was the object of Alex's irritation.

"I guess you and I can survive another audition." Leah tried to sound cheerful as she carefully positioned herself away from Alex's long legs and faced the barre for some pliés.

"The chance of dancing with Andrei Levintoff in a gala—with reporters and critics, Stephenson, makes this something more than 'another audition,'" Alex replied sharply. Leah bit her lip. Of course Alex would feel like that, considering how her heart was set on Andrei. Alex saw Leah's reflection in the mirror, and her expression softened slightly. "But I'd rather have you get it than that, that—" Alex gave up trying to compare Pam to anything worth mentioning.

It was a backhanded compliment, but Leah knew it was the best Alex could do—she was a proud girl who knew she was the best dancer currently enrolled in the school, outside of Leah. But Leah wasn't quite up to Alex's level yet: She was two years younger, without performing experience or the stamina that Alex possessed. No one at SFBA could possibly imagine anyone but Alex getting the part, and Leah knew that Alex would feel humiliated if she didn't. For Alex, this was a very important gala—she would probably leave the school next year, and most likely would have no trouble getting into a major company. Yet, even with her considerable talent, the honor of dancing with Andrei, as well as any positive reviews, would be very helpful to her career right now. Leah wondered aloud, "Why is Pam here?"

Alex again met her glance in the mirror and shrugged her shoulders. "Beats me!" A moment later Andrei walked in, followed by two boys from the school. Don Bryson, Pamela's latest partner, was one of them. He was older than Alex, and Leah didn't know him well. He lived in the Bay area in his own apartment, and was already auditioning for companies.

The other boy, Michael Litvak, walked right up to Leah. He had been her partner before she was paired up with James. After James's accident, Michael and Leah were assigned to work together again.

"So, today we learn the pas de deux from *La Bayadère*. The one with the scarf." Michael cracked his knuckles. Leah sometimes felt sorry for her tall, skinny partner. He was a talented dancer who just needed a few years to fill out and get stronger. He was a nervous sixteen-year-old with a rangy build. Leah had learned the only way to deal with him was to play down his fears. When they danced together, she forced herself to put aside her own trepidation and throw herself at him before he had a chance to worry that he might drop her. His lifts had improved greatly over the past month or so, and people were be-

ginning to talk about how well they moved together. Leah felt secretly pleased to know Michael's
improvement as a partner was due mainly to her.

"This should be fun," she said, forcing herself
to smile as she experimented with a couple of
posé turns, her hands on her hips. She couldn't
help but wonder why Andrei was bothering to
teach them the pas de deux, since Madame had
announced that he would partner the chosen girl
in a new piece created for the occasion.

"Okay, everyone," Andrei said. All conversation
stopped. Leah faced him and blushed a little when
his glance seemed to linger on her for a moment.
Today she had dressed with particular care. She
was wearing her favorite pair of turquoise stud
earrings that played up the blue of her large eyes.
Her black tank top leotard was the slinky kind
that clung to every curve. Leah was slender but
had a nice figure, and she couldn't help but wonder if Andrei had noticed. Then she remembered
Alex. She bit her lip and scolded herself for thinking of Andrei like that. Professional competition
is one thing, competing over Andrei is something
else, she repeated to herself over and over.

"Today," Andrei continued, "you probably think
what are all these people doing here." Andrei's
eyes seemed to settle on Alex a little, and Leah
caught the barest hint of a smile on his lips.
"Well, I think you boys can relax a little. None of
you will have the chance to be my partner."

Everyone in the room laughed loudly, and some
of the tension was broken.

"But I have chosen you three girls out of all the
others because you are all about the right size."

Leah's face fell, even though she knew he had a

point—whoever danced with Andrei couldn't be too tall. Alex was taller than Leah but still short enough to work with a guy Andrei's size. Pam was Leah's height but quite a bit heavier. Leah wondered if he could lift her, then remembered Pam's spectacular jump. A good jump helped during a lift. Besides, Andrei's arms looked very muscular.

"Because I watched you very carefully in the repertory class yesterday, I see you all are very strong dancers."

Leah's hopes soared just a little. At least being five foot four wasn't the only reason she was there.

"So, today I work with all of you. I understand none of you have danced the pas de deux from *La Bayadère* before, and I am sure you look forward to learning it."

To the right of Leah, Alex groaned.

Andrei heard her and laughed. "I just want to see how well we work together on this. I will see what the strength is of each girl. Though I am sure each one will inspire me to choreograph the new ballet, no?"

Leah just nodded. Once upon a time, picturing herself as inspiring the great Andrei Levintoff might have struck her as silly. Now it was so real it was almost scary.

Andrei worked a kink out of his powerful neck and went on. "I also teach the boys their part of the pas de deux. Madame says the ballet will be in the Bay Area company repertory soon, and you must all learn it anyway. If you go into the company in the next year or two, you should know it well by then. No matter who I choose, you will all continue to study this dance with your partner in class."

Andrei faced the students and called Alex. "Come here, little one; I will work with you first. You know parts of the piece already." Alex glowed with pleasure, and Leah was glad for her friend.

"What a charade this all is!" Pam grumbled as she stomped off to the rosin box. On her way back she hissed into Leah's ear. "I don't know why he bothers going through with it. Why doesn't he just call a spade a spade. Alex is his favorite because she is also Russian."

Leah gritted her teeth and deliberately stepped away from Pam. Of all things she disliked about the redhead, it was her caustic, biting tongue that sickened Leah most. On the other hand, a little voice inside of Leah couldn't help but agree. Why had Andrei made it seem as though there were a choice, when it was obvious the decision had already been made.

Leah and Michael tried to follow Andrei's lead. The pas de deux was very difficult. Not that Andrei expected them to learn the whole piece in one afternoon, but he chose certain sections. Of course, the part with the filmy scarf was one of them. Andrei distributed three lengths of pink polyester fabric. They looked like remnants from the company's wardrobe room. Leah had seen a videotape of the whole ballet once, and her favorite part had been the scarf scene, in which the danseur and the ballerina floated around the stage, each holding one end of a long piece of fabric. At one point the ballerina turned on pointe toward her partner, the scarf wrapping gracefully around her waist, then somehow she managed to turn away from him again gracefully, without getting tangled. Onstage the effect was breathtaking. In the classroom it was quite a different matter. Leah was convinced she'd be lucky if she left the class alive—she had the uncanny feeling that Michael would accidentally strangle her with the scarf.

After several attempts Leah still felt as if she, Michael, and the long scarf were on the verge of becoming entangled in a huge nasty knot. A warm hand landed on her shoulder. Leah looked up into Andrei's laughing eyes. "Here, Leah, let me show you. Watch, Michael. You hold the scarf like this." A minute later Leah was twirling herself into Andrei's arms. Somehow he made it all seem so easy.

"I think we will put the scarf away," he said, looking as if he was having trouble keeping a straight face. "That is enough for our first day of working on this. Now we do the last big lift. It is not easy, so please watch me carefully." This time he selected Leah first. She was conscious of Alex's eye on her, but did her best to concentrate and follow Andrei's instructions. He was talking mostly to Michael, but he demonstrated by having Leah mark the steps, gliding into the supported turns and leaping into the tricky lifts. Leah was surprised how comfortable it felt dancing with Andrei. The magic she'd felt with James just wasn't there. But there was something else—a poise, a sureness that inspired confidence and made it easy to look her best.

After Leah he chose Pam. It seemed perfectly natural at first. Andrei had worked with Alex about fifteen minutes, then fifteen more with Leah. Pam was next in line. But after fifteen minutes Andrei continued to work with Pam. Leah found her eyes riveted to the clock. Leah exchanged a glance with Alex, who was fuming.

"Can you believe this?" she murmured as Andrei continued dancing with Pam. "He hasn't looked at one of us for hours."

"For half an hour," Leah interjected, just to be fair.

Alex stomped toward the windows in disgust. Leah began to follow her when an anguished scream reverberated through the studio. *"Aaaaa-aaargh!"*

Leah wheeled around. Pam was crumpled in a heap on the floor, her right leg bent beneath her, her left at an awkward angle. "What happened?" Leah cried, horrified. For a split second Andrei stood stunned. Then he was on the floor by Pam's side. Tears were coursing down her face, and she was biting her lip hard. The girl was obviously in pain. For the first time since she'd met Pam, Leah actually felt sorry for her.

Michael and Don rushed over. Don and Andrei put their hands under her arms and tried to help her up.

"My knee," Pam wailed. "I can't put weight on it."

Leah went white. Knee injuries were always serious. Since she had been at the school, two girls had injured their knees, and one of them could never dance on pointe again, her ballet career over at sixteen. Leah didn't like Pam, but she knew Pam was talented and didn't deserve such a frightful injury.

"Try to walk on it a little," Andrei ordered,

taking charge. He made Pam lean on him. She limped painfully across the floor, then back again. She winced horribly, but with each step the going got easier.

"I do not think this is serious. But Michael and Don can help you downstairs. There is a therapist here, no?" He looked at Alex. She nodded numbly. Her face betrayed her mixed emotions. Pam getting knocked out right now meant Alex still had a chance to dance with Andrei at the gala. On the other hand, Alex looked afraid. When anyone got hurt at the Academy, the other girls' sympathy was often tinged with fear. As Leah went to the corner to fetch Pam's dance bag, she knew exactly what Alex was thinking because she was thinking it as well. What if it had been me?

She handed Pam's stuff to Michael and overheard Andrei talking to Pam. He spoke in a soft, gentle voice. "I am sure you will be okay soon. You are a strong girl. But I am sorry, Pam. I do not think you will be better in time for the gala." He stroked strands of her thick red hair off her tearstained cheeks, then tilted her face up so she would look him in the eye. "And I am sorry about that." He looked as if he was really hurting.

Leah wanted to believe she'd heard wrong. But the evidence was clear. Andrei had already decided that Pam would be working with him— something about her style obviously appealed to him. He must have liked working with her more than with Alex. Right then Leah made up her mind not to mention all this to Alex. He'd have to choose Alex now, she thought. Something inside her ached when she realized she hadn't ever really been in the running.

Andrei watched the boys help Pam out of the room. She wasn't crying anymore, and she held her head high. The door to the practice room closed, and Andrei stood watching it a moment more. Then he shook his head as if to clear his thoughts and glanced up at the clock. "I think, girls, we have danced enough for today. Tomorrow I will share my decision with you. Come back here tomorrow to this studio, at about four P.M." He didn't look at either Alex or Leah as he spoke. Grabbing a towel from the barre, he shouldered his bag and left the studio.

Alex ran after him. "Wait, Andrei," she said breathlessly. "About tonight ..." The words floated back into the room, then the door closed behind them.

Leah stood in the middle of the dance floor, relieved that Alex had left. She would have been too tempted to share her discovery. Andrei had already decided on Pam, and if it weren't for the accident, neither Leah nor Alex would have had a chance.

Chapter 6

Leah sat on the living room floor,
her fists clenched inside the pockets of her favorite purple overalls. The sun was setting behind the hills, and the bright, late afternoon light washed through Mrs. Hanson's antique lace curtains, setting off what seemed like sparks from Pamela Hunter's fiery hair. Leah was trying hard to be nice to Pam, as were most of the other boarders. Though Pam's injury didn't threaten her career, it still hurt, and beneath her makeup she looked pale. Leah was pretty sure it wasn't just the pain in her knee that had Pamela feeling down—she had just missed out on her first real career break. Most likely, after the gala, no SFBA student would ever have the chance to dance with Andrei Levintoff again. The awful part was knowing that another girl was always there, right behind you, ready to step in. As much as Leah disliked Pam, she felt sorry for her. The Student Matinee was a major event, and Pam would have been the star of it if it had not been for this accident. Leah had

never been injured—just the thought of putting herself in Pam's place made her stomach quiver.

Leah, Suzanne, and Melanie sat in a semicircle at Pam's feet, and though Pam had muted the sound of the television with the remote, Suzanne and Melanie had their eyes glued to "M*A*S*H," while Leah was preoccupied with her kitten. Misha was curled in Pam's lap, sound asleep. Leah felt betrayed by her own cat. Since he had moved into the boardinghouse, he had singled out Pam as his best friend. Leah was annoyed because she missed the time when he had slept with her at night, and also because he made her wonder if he knew something about Pamela that no one else did. Leah forced herself to look away from Misha, over toward Alex, who sat at the piano. Leah admired the tall, dark girl as she played a rather difficult Rachmaninoff etude.

"Of course, I will dance again," Pam said, her voice straining to be heard over the heavy progression of arpeggios and chords. With an exaggerated sigh she slowly shifted her position amid the sea of cushions and pillows on which she sat. She reached out her hand as Abigail presented her with a mug of steamy, fragrant tea, Mrs. Hanson's famous herbal cure-all, which Leah knew from experience tended to soothe you inside and out. Pam took a sip and handed the mug back to Abigail. After glancing at Alex to be sure she was listening, she delivered what she obviously intended to be a lethal blow. "And to think I was going to be Andrei Levintoff's partner—and now this rotten bit of luck."

The music broke off abruptly. Alex spun around on the piano stool. "How do you come to that conclusion, Pamela?" Alex snapped, with a proud toss of her dark hair.

Pam whipped her head around and gave Leah a penetrating stare. "You tell her, Stephenson. You heard what Andrei said, didn't you?"

Leah felt confused, but decided to hold her ground. Pam was out of the running, and there was no point in hurting Alex with what was now meaningless information. "I didn't hear him say you'd be his partner."

The phone rang, and Leah was closest to it. Grateful for the timely interruption, she picked up before the second ring. "Hello!" she said. "Oh, yes, of course." She cupped her hand over the receiver. "Someone for you. He's got a Russian accent, but it's not Andrei," she said, passing the phone to Alex.

Alex's moodiness vanished as quickly as it had come. She curled her legs up under her on the stool and spoke into the phone, smiling brilliantly. "Father!" she cried without even saying hello. "I thought you had forgotten about tonight—yes, yes, of course he will come. We are to pick him up at seven at Patrick's apartment. I will. I know they'll both love meeting you."

Alex hung up the phone and motioned for Leah to follow her into the hall. Kay had just come out of the kitchen, holding a bowl of salad in her hand. Alex stopped her from joining the others in the living room. "My parents just phoned. Do you want to have dinner with them? Both of you are invited."

"Are you kidding?" Leah's eyes opened very wide. "Your parents are here, in San Francisco?"

Alex grinned her assent.

"Do you mean Kay and I will actually get to spend the evening with Olga and Dimitri Sorokin?"

"Yeah, my mom and dad," Alex said in perfect mimicry of Leah's California accent.

"Tonight?" Kay's voice emerged from her throat, sounding like a squeak. "Tell me it's not tonight!" She tugged anxiously on the shirttails hanging out of her jeans.

"Sure. They'll be here about seven. We'll pick up Andrei and—"

"Andrei?" Leah found herself blushing. She bent down and retied the laces of her Reeboks. The prospect of dinner with Alex *and* Andrei after her encounter the night before on the Alvarezes' terrace unnerved Leah.

"Of course," Alex said a trifle sharply. "Remember, he's a family friend." Leah's color was back to normal by the time she straightened up. She even managed to tease Alex. "I don't think 'family friend' is the right word for it."

Alex looked pleased at Leah's joke and continued. "So, if we are to leave at seven, you'd better both get changed and—" Alex broke off in midsentence. "What's wrong, Kay?"

Kay looked crestfallen. She stood in the doorway of the kitchen looking as if she was trying very hard not to cry. "I can't go out with you and your parents." Her voice cracked a little, but finally she managed to explain. "Because—now this is supposed to be a secret—but Johnny told me Madame wants my ballet to be in the gala."

"What!" Leah and Alex cried in unison.

Alex threw her arms around Kay and gave her a hug. "What incredible news, Kay. I'm so happy for you."

Kay seemed anything but happy. "But we have a rehearsal tonight at the school." Her voice grew even more miserable. "Why do things like this always happen to me? Your dad is one of my all-time favorite dancers!" She rubbed her nose with the sleeve of her baggy flannel shirt and sniffed loudly.

"He'll be back again," Leah tried to soothe Kay, looking to Alex for confirmation; but Alex grimaced.

"They don't often end up in San Francisco. They're stopping on their way to Japan to kick off a Far Eastern tour. But next time," Alex hastily added, "I promise, you can go out with us."

Kay brightened slightly.

"Besides," Alex teased, "having your ballet in the Matinee is much more important than dinner with the Sorokin family, though you haven't told any of us a thing about your secret project."

"You've been so hush-hush." Turning to Alex, Leah spoke in a stage whisper, "Should I leak this news to the press?"

"How can you? Kay Larkin *is* the press around here." Alex laughed.

Kay blushed with pride and already looked a little less upset about missing dinner with the internationally renowned Sorokins. "You have to be secretive about this kind of thing. Madame said it had to be a surprise. Besides, Johnny Cullum says that if you talk about what you're doing too much, you lose the inspiration to really do it."

"Well, whatever you do, I think we're all going to be pretty proud of you when you come out for curtain calls in the Opera House. Kay Larkin's debut as a great choreographer, and to think I

was there!" Leah said dramatically. And proud
she would be, too. Until recently, Kay's reputation
at SFBA was that of a talented but not very dedi-
cated student. Now that she had begun to deal
with her feelings about her mother, Kay was working much harder, making use of the potential
previously ignored when she was feeling confused about her mother. Leah also suspected her
spate of hard work had something to do with her
passion for creating ballets rather than just dancing them. Rumor had it that Kay had a considerable gift as a choreographer, and Madame's
selecting Kay's latest effort to be part of the gala
was proof of that.

Later that evening Leah found herself in the
seat of honor at a large corner table of the Happy
Clam, the chic Sausalito restaurant that boasted a
wide array of seafood, a select clientele, and floor-
to-ceiling windows overlooking San Francisco Bay.
The fog erased the contours of the lumpy hills
and blurred the lights on the Golden Gate Bridge.
Any other evening Leah would have sat entranced
by the strange, misty view. But that night Leah might
as well have been facing a brick wall, she found
the company so fascinating. On one side of her
was Andrei, and on the other was Dimitri Sorokin.
Olga, Alex's mother, sat across from her, and Alex
was tucked between her mother and Andrei.

Leah had been afraid she'd feel out of her ele-
ment with Andrei and the Sorokins. After all, Alex's
parents seemed so polished and sophisticated,
being famous international stars. She wondered
what in the world she would talk about with
them. Debating with herself for half an hour, she

finally came to a decision about what to wear. Because of the cool, damp weather, she had settled for slim wool pants and her favorite sweater, a fuzzy pink one that brought out the color in her cheeks.

The Sorokins had surprised her—especially Olga, Alex's mother, who insisted on being called by her first name. She was tall and dark and could have been Alex's older sister. She wore a lovely red-and-cream silk scarf tied around her upswept hair, and her cream-colored pants were topped with a scarlet sweater. She was dressed every bit as casually as Leah, sharing Leah's love of bright colors. Olga was warm and talkative and put Leah at ease. No one spoke Russian, and though Leah had braced herself for a difficult evening, to her surprise she found herself feeling right at home.

"It is wonderful for Alexandra," Alex's father was saying, as the waiter cleared away the entree dishes before passing out dessert menus, "that you came to study at the San Francisco Ballet Academy."

"Well it's great for me that Alex is here," Leah responded warmly, grinning at Alex. "She and Kay are my two best friends."

"Yes, I'm sorry we didn't get to meet Kay this time," Olga Sorokin remarked, looking up from the menu. "Alexandra says she is lots of fun and very talented."

"Which girl is Kay?" Andrei inquired.

"The short one!" Leah and Alex replied in unison, bursting into laughter.

"See, that is what I mean," said Dimitri Sorokin to his wife. "You know, Alexandra used to be much too serious."

Alex rolled her eyes toward the ceiling. "Faaaather!" she wailed in protest.

Leah laughed again. Somehow she had never expected the Sorokins to act like a normal family. Alex actually felt embarrassed by her parents when they treated her like a child, as would any other American teenager Leah knew. She filed the information away to share with Kay.

"But Dimitri is right." Andrei turned to face Leah. "Making a friend in a new place is a very important thing, no?" He spoke with such warmth that Leah began to feel uncomfortable. Before she had a chance to recover her composure, Andrei made everything ten times worse. Speaking to the Sorokins, he said, "Leah is the first friend I have made here, too. We talked a long time last night about many things no one else seems to understand."

"What do you mean?" Alex immediately asked, sitting up straight in her chair.

Leah's back stiffened at the sharpness of her tone.

Andrei was oblivious to the tension he'd just created. He went on in an eager, happy voice, "Even back home there were no dancers who understood how much I miss the farm, living where things grow and it is so alive."

"That's right. Leah's a farm girl. I had almost forgotten."

Leah gaped at Alex. That was the sort of remark Pam Hunter would make. Leah would never forget the time Pamela had made a similar comment, insulting her in front of James during audition week. She had made being born in San Lorenzo, California, sound like a worse fate than

waking up with a wart on the middle of your
nose. Leah bristled—Alex was making Leah feel
the same way now, self-conscious and naive. Leah
had a pretty good idea why she was acting so
spiteful. Alex's motives could be summed up in a
word. Andrei. Leah knew that Alex was jealous of
Andrei's attention toward her, but was that any
excuse to say hurtful things to a friend?

Snatches of the Sorokins' conversation with
Andrei drifted toward Leah: something about a
farm, Andrei's upcoming season with American
Ballet Theatre next May ... Leah only half took in
what they were saying. Andrei's dream farm and
his career plans didn't interest her. Her friendship
with Alex concerned her right now, particularly
the fact that Alex didn't trust her. Maybe Leah
had mentally betrayed Alex last night, but when it
came right down to it, she was perfectly loyal.
She would never, ever, flirt with a guy who was
seeing one of her friends. Never! she fumed inwardly. And she'd tell Alex that later, in no uncertain terms.

Andrei draped his arm around Leah's shoulder
and gave her an affectionate squeeze. "But the
point is, my friends, that I have found someone in
the world of ballet who understands me! Someone who does not think wanting to live on a farm
is a silly idea. Not like this one here," he said,
pinching Alex's cheek as if she were a five-year-
old. "She thinks Andrei is a simple country boy
who does not know how lucky he is to dance and
live in big cities and have everything his heart
desires."

At that moment Leah wished the San Andreas
fault would open and swallow her. That way, Andrei

would have to shut up about the bond he felt with Leah, and Alex wouldn't have time to worry about Leah's loyalty. But Leah had learned long ago that earthquakes and other natural disasters were never very obliging. Alex looked terribly upset and became only more agitated as Andrei failed to remove his arm from Leah's shoulders. When it was more than she could take, Alex stood abruptly, excusing herself to search for the ladies' room. When Andrei finally did withdraw his arm, Leah was surprised how disappointed she was, and how empty she felt.

"Leah Stephenson, you certainly have a way of making things complicated!" Alex declared later that night, back at the boardinghouse.

Leah tried to glare at Alex, but it was hard. In spite of her anger, Leah was tempted to laugh. Alex looked so ridiculous, smearing globs of green clay on her already porcelain-smooth face in front of the bathroom mirror. Her luxuriant black hair was plastered on top of her head, midway through her weekly hot-oil treatment. Not rain, not snow, not love, not the wrath of a friend, could distract Alex from her pursuit of what she called "naturally clean and healthy good looks." Leah was sure Alex had picked up that phrase from a fashion magazine, because Alex didn't give the impression of being the "natural" type at all. Makeup, dramatic jewelry, and her exclusively black or all-white wardrobe gave Alex a very sophisticated look. Sultry, even sexy, were words Leah would use to describe Alex, but never natural.

Leah sat on the edge of the tub, wishing there were some way to get through to her friend. But

Alex was an escape artist—at least when it came to avoiding confrontations that she wasn't in the mood for.

The trouble was, Leah couldn't figure out why Alex was in such a good mood, taking such pains to pretend that nothing bad had happened at the Happy Clam.

Leah sighed and decided to try one more time to get through to her. "Alex, I'm not making mountains out of molehills, or blowing things out of proportion. I just felt hurt tonight."

"Because I said you were from a farm?" Alex sounded very righteous.

Leah stuck to her guns. Alex meant so much to her—she just *had* to understand what Leah was saying. "Because of *how* you said I was from a farm."

"Really, Leah," Alex scoffed, arching one eyebrow at Leah's reflection in the mirror. The carefully applied green mask cracked a little as Alex scowled. She dipped her finger in a pot of imported French clay and dabbed at the fissure in her mask. For the second time that night Leah thought about earthquakes—she wished something would come along and shake her friend up so she'd open her eyes and see that there really was some kind of problem between them.

Leah tried a different tack. "Okay, forget about the farm, though you did hurt me. I just thought it was important that we discuss it."

Alex groaned through her teeth so as not to disturb the rapidly drying mask.

Leah ignored her and went on. "What has me upset is the fact that you are jealous, and you won't admit it and—"

"Jealous?" Alex chuckled and tried not to move her lips. "Why would I be jealous?"

"Because of Andrei, and the way he said we were friends." Even as she said that, Leah realized how flat the words sounded.

"But I *am* glad you are friends," Alex said turning around to face Leah. "He needs friends here. People to talk to. Especially since—" Alex cut herself off and faced the sink. She turned on the water full force and tested it with her hand. As soon as she judged it to be the right temperature, she began splashing her face with it, washing the mud away.

Leah kept on talking over the noise of the running water. "Why didn't you finish it? Especially since you and he aren't just friends?" Leah doubted Alex could hear her, but was startled when Alex turned around, caked patches of green clay lingering on her face.

"Exactly, Leah," Alex said firmly. "I told you before. Andrei is no longer just a friend. Since he has come into my life, he has changed everything."

With great effort Leah restrained herself from asking Alex exactly what had changed in the past couple of days. Outside of Pam's injury nothing much had happened, and certainly nothing had in Alex's life unless ... Leah suddenly remembered their leaving the Happy Clam an hour or so before. Andrei had gone off alone with Alex, and while Leah had talked to Dimitri and Olga, they had walked together along the breakwater, their figures barely distinguishable in the fog. When they turned up at the car, Alex was glowing. "He told you, didn't he?" Leah asked more calmly than she felt. "You'll be dancing with him in the gala."

Alex stood up very tall and clutched her silky white robe tight at the neck. "He did not. He hasn't made up his mind yet, and even if he had, he wouldn't tell me first."

Leah scrutinized Alex's face. She looked a little strange—half her face mask on, and half washed off—and *very* indignant. No, Alex wasn't lying—she was good at avoiding things, but she never told a lie. "I'm sorry," Leah apologized. "I jumped to conclusions. I just couldn't figure out why you looked so happy when you came back to the car."

Alex smiled as if she had a very special secret. "That's okay. But ..." Alex sat down on the tub next to Leah. "It is just that ..." She sounded a little embarrassed. "Oh, Leah," she finally blurted out. "He is in love with me."

Leah's eyes grew big. "Andrei told you he loves you?"

"Not those words exactly," Alex hedged, "but he said it makes him very happy to be with me, and he's not lonely anymore the way he was when he first left home."

Leah relaxed a little. Alex wasn't jealous of her now—she didn't have to be. "I'm glad he said that," she said earnestly, squeezing Alex's arm. "I really am." She was also glad there was still the ghost of a chance that Andrei hadn't yet written her off—as a partner.

Chapter 7

I must be dreaming! Leah thought.

The next afternoon, Leah had come to the west studio to endure Andrei's verdict. But then, she must have heard wrong, or maybe she was really still asleep at Mrs. Hanson's, beneath her downy quilt in her very own bed. Just to be sure, she pinched herself and realized she *was* awake. Suddenly her heart was thumping at twice its normal speed. She looked up and met Andrei's pure-blue eyes. He was looking down at her, smiling, wiping the sweat from his face with a towel.

"Well, Leah, now it is time to start rehearsing, no?" Andrei said, tossing the towel across the room.

"But where's Alex?" Leah hadn't wanted to ask, but the question just slipped out. It just didn't make sense—Alex had been trained in Russia, and supposedly they were in love with each other. At that moment Leah didn't know how she'd ever face Alex again.

"Alex will perform other dances." Andrei made it sound so simple. Alex had said the same thing herself a million times. Sometimes Leah would land the big roles, sometimes Alex would. The trick was to stay friends through it all, to put injured pride aside and remember that there would be times of triumph for both of them. But Alex didn't have Andrei in mind when she had said all that. Andrei was different—not because Leah would get to appear with him in the Student Matinee—but because Alex was in love with him.

Leah didn't realize that Andrei had been standing so close to her until he walked away. Finally Andrei returned to her side. "You must not worry about Alex. Please. This pas de deux is for you and me to dance together." He took her arm and led her to the center of the floor. He sat down and motioned for her to sit down next to him; the word "together" was still running through her head.

Andrei started rehearsal by talking her through the steps. "Debussy's *Prelude to the Afternoon of a Faun* is the music for this ballet."

Leah's face lit up. "That's one of my favorite pieces!"

Andrei nodded enthusiastically and flashed her a warm smile. "I had a feeling you would like it. It is mine, too." Raking his fingers through his longish hair, he closed his eyes and tried to gather his thoughts. "Some of the parts I have already worked out. But I have to choreograph some of it on us—the way you move will have a lot to do with this ballet. Some people make dances in their heads first. I think of the dancers as helping me create the dance."

Leah was thrilled. Suddenly she didn't feel as passive anymore. Working out a new ballet with

Andrei meant she didn't just have to do what she was told and perform the same steps a hundred other ballerinas had performed in the past in exactly the same way. She could be herself, because the dance would be tailor-made for her. That pleased Leah immensely.

"Maybe you have seen another ballet performed to this music. But this will be different. It has to do with a boy and a girl, but it will be more abstract. Now, sometimes one person's loneliness touches another person's loneliness. Remember when we talked under the stars?"

Leah's heart almost stopped. How could she forget?

"At the beginning of the ballet, it is about making a friend. As for love, it is something that develops over time."

Leah felt a strange new sensation course up her spine. Andrei was making his choreography so personal. A voice deep inside of Leah prodded her to remember Alex, but as Andrei talked, the warning grew dimmer.

"But words do not make a dance," said Andrei, scrambling to his feet.

Leah suddenly felt awkward. No one had choreographed a dance on her before. She knew it was a real privilege, perhaps an even greater privilege than being partnered by Andrei in the Matinee. No matter who danced this ballet again, it would be shaped by her movement, as if she had somehow left her fingerprint on the numerous combinations. Andrei had said he would have to work the way Leah Stephenson moved best. As Andrei motioned for her to move to a far corner of the room and explained how to begin, Leah couldn't help but wonder what he would have done with Pam. They moved so differently from each other. All at once Leah was acutely aware that she was Andrei's second choice.

But worries about Pam and Alex soon vanished from her mind. She was too busy concentrating on Andrei's instructions. The combinations were difficult and almost awkward for her at first. Andrei's way of putting things together surprised her, but after the first few minutes of struggling with a particular sequence or lift, the movement became easier; and Leah began to enjoy the feeling of dancing something no one had ever danced before. The harder Andrei pushed her, the harder she worked. In spite of his difficulties with the language, he expressed himself wonderfully with wide, expansive gestures. Alex had told Leah he painted as a hobby, and she could believe it. He definitely thought in pictures rather than words, as did Leah herself. Leah felt comfortable with him, as if she had been dancing with him her whole life. He made everything Leah was supposed to do so incredibly clear.

"Open the arms, so—" he stated at one point, "and feel as if you are longing for your partner. Even if there is no real story here, make one up in your head. You have not seen the man of your dreams for a long time. You want to be beautiful for him, from your toes to your fingertips. Leah, imagine there are flowers growing on the ends of your fingers, because you are enchanted. Maybe you are a girl who bursts into blossom when she stands in the moonlight. There is a story of a woman who is touched by the man who loves her, and she becomes a tree. Imagine the leaves that are growing out of your fingers, and there is a cool spring wind blowing in your hair."

As Andrei warned, his ballet had no real story. The ballet itself was more of a mood, a lonely yet beautiful mood. The steps suggested two people who accidentally touch each other before drifting back into their own separate worlds. Andrei's images inspired Leah as she'd never been inspired before. Yet, there were no currents of electricity or moments when time stopped. It was a grueling cycle, mainly hard work and concentration and counting the complex rhythms. Yet his choreography began to feel increasingly natural to her, and tired as she was, the rehearsal was over way too soon. When the music stopped Leah felt confused, as if she had just awakened from a dream.

The haunting Debussy melody seemed to be coursing through her veins, and as she walked into the dressing room, she was still envisioning the steps she'd just learned.

"Are you satisfied?" Alex practically spat at her.

Leah looked up and froze. Alex was dressed in tight black pants and a turtleneck. Her coat was over one arm and she looked damp, as if she'd just come in from outdoors. Her full lips were turned down and her brow was furrowed in an angry frown.

"Alex, I'm sorry you didn't get the part. I really am," Leah said from the bottom of her heart. She knew how proud Alex was and that she must tread softly for the sake of their friendship. She tried to push back the vision of Andrei in her mind, the way he inspired her, and how natural it felt to put her hand in his and twirl across the room with him, as if they were indeed two people whose loneliness had touched for a time.

"Oh, Leah, stop being so noble about it." Alex threw her coat down and crossed her arms across her chest. Two little red spots burned on her usually pale cheeks. "You pretend to be so good, so innocent, so above it all when it comes to the competitive backbiting games people play around here. You even had me fooled." Alex let out a hard, brittle laugh. "You're a real—what is that word Kay loves? You're a real champ!"

She stomped over to the studio door, then back again, pausing only to kick a battered-looking toe shoe under the bench.

Leah had always suspected an angry Alex was someone she'd prefer to avoid. Now she was the object of Alex's fury, and she was scared. Struggling to stay calm, Leah declared, "Alex, I don't know what you're talking about. Andrei told us he'd choose one of us today. He chose me, and that's all there is to it." Leah's voice rose slightly. "I don't know what you're implying, but I resent it. Either one of us could have gotten this part. I don't know why he preferred me over you, but it's his right, you know. You don't own him!" Leah concluded hotly. She glared angrily at Alex. Where was Alex's brave talk now, about staying friends no matter who got what roles?

"You don't know why he chose you?" Alex's eyebrows shot up. "Listen, Stephenson, I was there last night. I saw with my very own eyes." She tapped her chest, shaking a finger in Leah's face. "I saw the way you played up to Andrei, batting your big blue eyes at him, trying to steal him from me." Alex glared at Leah, then abruptly turned around. She made a noise that sounded very much as if she were choking back her tears.

"Trying to do what?" Leah cried, astounded by Alex's accusation.

"Steal him. Do I have to spell it out?"

"No," Leah retorted, furious. "You don't, but last night when I tried to talk to you about being jealous, you pretended you didn't know what I was talking about. I told you then, and I'll tell you again, now. I would never, ever, even think of stealing a guy from one of my friends," Leah said indignantly. "I'm not interested in Andrei, not that way," Leah asserted, dimly aware that she wasn't quite telling the truth. "And if anyone's acting two-faced around here, it's you, Alexandra. You're just disappointed about the part, so it's very convenient to accuse me of stealing the guy you love. Well, Andrei chose me because he wanted to dance with me, not because he wants to go out with me." Leah tore off her sweaty black leotard and peeled off her tights. She turned her back on Alex, and rummaged in her bag for a white container of baby powder. She sprinkled it over herself before reaching for her clothes.

Alex tapped her foot sharply against the grimy linoleum floor. Her eyes bored into Leah, as if she were trying to peer into the depth of her soul. Leah couldn't help but squirm under her gaze. Leah knew she hadn't come on to Andrei to get the part—she had actually given up on getting it. But she couldn't swear she hadn't been flirting with him last night. The effect Andrei had on her made it hard to be sure of anything.

Alex's next accusation took Leah totally off guard. "Or maybe you always hold hands in the moonlight with guys you're not interested in. Really, Leah, I didn't think that was your style." Though Alex sounded scornful, she looked really hurt.

Leah stood frozen to the spot. She had just pulled her sweater over her head, but she couldn't force her arms through the sleeves. She could only stare at Alex, dumbfounded. "What are you talking about?" she asked, though she had a sinking feeling in her stomach because she knew what Alex would say next.

Leah blushed guiltily. Pam. Pam had spilled the beans about Andrei kissing her on the veranda. It had only been a friendly gesture on his part, but Leah couldn't swear right now that her feelings were just friendly toward Andrei. Not after this rehearsal and the feeling of friendship they shared, on the dance floor and under the stars. He had been so intimate, so personal, when he talked to her about his new dance.

Alex looked like a cat about to pounce. "I heard all about your sneaking off with him at Mrs. Alvarez's house and kissing him on the veranda. Everyone's talking about it. It felt horrible to have someone come to me and tell me what my best friend's been doing behind my back."

Alex's accusation suddenly brought Leah to her senses. Having feelings about Andrei was one thing, but she hadn't encouraged him. And that kiss was just friendly. And if Alex wanted to believe the worst of her, well, that was Alex's tough luck.

Leah drew herself up very tall and spoke in a shrill but steady voice. "Listen Alex, if you want to believe a malicious girl like Pam, that's your business. I don't care," she said with great dignity. "I wasn't stealing Andrei from you. I was just talking to him. And yes, he kissed me, but it was a friendly sort of kiss. It meant nothing. And it certainly had nothing in the world to do with getting this part." Then Leah remembered something very important. "In fact, Madame hadn't even announced the gala until after Pam saw us out there. Did it ever occur to you that Pam didn't see fit to tell you about it until she was out of the running?" Leah paused and then challenged Alex. "But if you don't want to believe me, why don't you ask him yourself? He's still in the studio working on the piece. Go out there and talk to Andrei. Get him to tell you why he gave me the part instead of you."

Alex looked surprised at Leah's suggestion. She hesitated only a second. "Okay, I will do just that." With her head held high, Alex marched into the studio and slammed the dressing room door in Leah's face.

Leah's common sense told her not to listen, but she was too angry to heed her conscience. She pulled on her jeans, and brushed her hair. Then she sat down on the dressing room bench and pressed her ear to the thin wall.

Alex went right to the point. "I have something to say to you, Andrei Levintoff."

"Now, Alex," Andrei soothed. His voice was low, but Leah could make out most of his words. "I am sorry about your not getting the part, but I can explain."

"Explain?" Alex shouted. "Explain what? That our friendship means nothing, or that everything you said to me last night means nothing?"

"Alex, you are not being fair. I did not mention

this ballet last night. Last night was a beautiful evening with friends, no? It had nothing to do with work here. Nothing," he emphasized.

"No," Alex said unreasonably, "you didn't mention this ballet or your decision. You didn't on purpose. I had to find out through the grapevine that you chose Leah. Why Andrei, why?" The pain in Alex's voice cut through Leah's anger, leaving her feeling as unhappy as Alex.

"Why did I choose Leah?" Andrei repeated, surprised at the question.

Alex's response startled Leah. "No, I'm asking you why you didn't tell me first. I feel like such a fool." Leah heard the sound of something heavy dropping to the ground. She peeked through a crack in the wall. Alex had plunked herself down in the middle of the dance floor. She was sitting with her legs spread out, chewing on a strand of her thick dark hair. Her usually straight back was slumped a little, and she looked very young and vulnerable. Andrei sat down next to her. There was a short distance between them. But it might as well have been a hundred miles.

Andrei reached out and tried to tilt her chin so he could see her face. Alex leapt up and turned her back on him. Leah could see her bottom lip trembling.

"I tried to find you before this rehearsal. I wanted to tell you then," Andrei pleaded for her to understand. "But you were not anywhere I looked. I thought, then, you would come here, like I asked you yesterday. But you did not come. You cannot blame me for that." He was beginning to sound a little angry now.

Alex ground the heel of her boot into the floor.

Madame would kill her if she saw her on the dance floor with her street shoes, Leah thought absently.

Alex turned to face Andrei, tears running down her face. "Why didn't you pick me?"

Taking a few steps away from her, Andrei pounded the fist of one hand into the palm of the other. He seemed to debate with himself for a moment, then his shoulders heaved and he sighed deeply. "I should not tell you this, but Madame and the people who direct the school did not want me to choose a Russian girl. They thought it would not make the sponsors happy. They thought it was important that I dance with a young American student. That is why I wanted Pam."

Alex's shriek filled the room. "Pamela Hunter!" Alex gaped in disbelief at Andrei. "You were going to pick *her*?" Alex took a few angry strides back toward the dressing room. Leah cringed, starting to get up. She didn't want Alex to catch her listening, but Alex suddenly stopped and turned. She wasn't finished with Andrei just yet. She marched back to him, planting her hands on her slim hips. She stared up at Andrei, disgust evident in her face. "Leah is one thing. She is a gifted dancer. I can accept that, though I am still angry with you—" Alex cut herself off and averted her eyes before she went on. "But Pam—she is a terrible dancer."

Andrei surprised Leah by leaping to Pam's defense. "No, she is not terrible. She is very good— perfect technique and a strong quality that I like. Never have I seen a girl who jumps like her. I think she would have danced very well in my ballet. Like an earth goddess. Leah will be good, too. She will give it a different feeling. More like spring or a girl new to love. She looks very young and innocent."

Hearing that description, Leah cursed under her breath and vowed to change the way she dressed.

"But Pam was the girl I wanted," Andrei said with a certainty that could not be disputed.

Alex fell silent for a moment. "I think you're crazy. But I can't believe our dumb school Matinee has to be cast to please the contributors. It's not fair, and it's bad artistic policy. I hate it." Alex said vehemently. "Where one is born has nothing, absolutely nothing, to do with how they can dance."

Andrei said something to Alex, and she looked up at him, still suspicious. He said something else, and only then did Leah realize he was speaking Russian.

Alex turned away from him, but he continued to talk to her anyway in a low, soothing tone. Then he began to massage her shoulders. Slowly, slowly, a smile came to Alex's lips. She leaned back against him ever so slightly, then she turned around and put her arms around his neck and said something back.

Watching them Leah felt a curious empty feeling in the pit of her stomach. A tear spilled out of Leah's eye, and as she wiped it away, she noticed she was crying. She tossed her head proudly, in a way that said "What difference does it make to me?" and stopped looking through the hole in the wall. There was no point in listening anymore. Besides, eavesdropping had done little for her ego.

She was dancing with Andrei at the gala Matinee only because Pam was hurt and she was the only American left in the running. What a low blow! Leah leaned against the wall, disgusted with herself for having looked out the peephole. She gnawed her lower lip and hugged her arms against her chest, slowly rocking back and forth. What a fool she was to have believed that she was dancing with the great Russian star because she was someone special. Because she had something none of the other girls had, some particular talent, some grace, some way of moving that made her unique.

For the first time since she'd come to SFBA, Leah felt as if she were second-rate. At that thought she let out a low, bitter laugh. No, not second-rate, but third. She felt as if someone had just pulled the earth out from under her feet. How could she have been so stupid all these months to believe that she was the best dancer in the school? Diana had once said that she wasn't. Leah hadn't wanted to believe her then, but now the evidence was overwhelming.

Andrei, of course, would have preferred to dance with Alex. But since he needed an American partner, he had chosen Pamela Hunter—Leah's nemesis! Diana had always said Pam was more talented than Leah and would go farther. Why hadn't Leah listened to her? She wouldn't be feeling so awful now if she'd been more realistic. Of course, Leah was lucky. Everyone said that. This time Leah's luck led to Pam's getting hurt; and the prize part in the gala landed at her feet. Well, the idea of dancing with Andrei Levintoff right now didn't seem like much of a prize at all. Leah sat very straight and still, trying to maintain emotional control. She had never felt so insulted in her whole life. There was only one thing to do. March in there right now and tell Andrei she wouldn't dance the part after all, thereby handing it over to Alex, just as he had wanted to in the first place. If Leah backed out now, he'd have every excuse in the world to dance with his girlfriend.

Leah got up, shouldered her bag, and started toward the door leading back into the studio. Peals of laughter filtered into the dressing room, and Leah stopped to listen to the strains of a lively Russian folk tune coming from the studio. Alex and Andrei must have turned on the tape deck. She heard some clapping, floor stomping, and the clatter of Alex's high heeled boots. Alex laughed and Andrei let out a cheerful yelp. They sounded so vigorous and alive that Leah found herself tapping her foot in time with them. The music was like a spell made to set your feet to dancing.

She listened for a moment longer, tempted to go in and watch. But she decided not to, though she was completely caught up in their enthusiasm. She didn't feel angry or insulted anymore—something about the music had lifted her spirits. She didn't really want to make a scene. And she had a strong sense that giving up the part was something she would live to regret. But even though she felt uplifted by the music, she still felt hurt welling up in the depths of her being. Andrei hadn't chosen her because of her dancing ability. Her dancing with Andrei was a political decision and nothing more.

Leah stole out of the dressing room quietly and hurried down the stairs. She had no idea how long Andrei's music would last, and she was too upset to face Alex just yet. Besides, she felt slighted on another score. While she had been dancing with Andrei, she had imagined he had felt something special for her—not just as a dancer, but as a girl.

Leah stood in the kitchen that night, her arms submerged up to the elbows in dirty dishwater. She had volunteered for kitchen duty to avoid the usual after-dinner socializing in the living room. She didn't want to have to face Alex. Dinner had been bad enough—at least for Leah. She didn't feel like talking to Alex, or eating, for that matter. The trouble was that Alex didn't seem upset at all.

A tear rolled down Leah's cheek and plopped into the sudsy water.

"Leah?" Alex called her name, causing Leah to jump.

Leah responded through clenched teeth, "What do you want?"

Alex leaned against the counter trying to look at Leah's downcast face. "I thought we had—what is the phrase—a deal?"

Leah whirled around, not quite able to believe her ears. "A deal?" she repeated scornfully. "What kind of deal?" Leah purposely turned back to her dishes and began scrubbing the roasting pan with all her might to vent her pent-up emotions.

"Come on, Leah," Alex coaxed, reaching over and shutting off the water. "Look at me. I'm sorry about today."

Leah met her glance and held it, expelling a sigh. She shook her head, unable to accept her friend's attempts to apologize. "Alex, you accused me of some pretty nasty things today and I—" Leah started out sounding quite self-righteous, but then she remembered eavesdropping and how much it had hurt seeing Alex put her arms around Andrei. "It doesn't matter now," she said in a small, defeated voice.

"But it does," Alex insisted, pushing her over to a kitchen chair. "It really does. I am sorry for hurting you, but you know I have my pride. I took it for granted that Andrei would choose me—for a lot of reasons." Alex surprised Leah with another one of her secret smiles. "But he wanted you, and now I have to accept that."

"I guess you do," Leah said, still smarting from Alex's earlier outburst.

"And this round went to you, but you'd better beware next time," Alex threatened with a grin.

Leah tried to remain angry with her friend, but she just couldn't. She loved sparring with Alex. "Okay. We'll see what happens next time."

The kitchen door squeaked open, and Andrei poked his golden head in. "My two muses!" He strode into the kitchen and stood with one hand on the back of Alex's chair, and the other on Leah's.

"Andrei, what are you doing here?" Alex jumped up and threw her arms around his neck. He hugged her back before stepping away.

"I think it is time to try your favorite place to get fat!" He patted Alex's flat tummy and made a gallant effort to pinch some excess fat around his waist, though, of course, there was none. He was all muscle, sinew, and bone.

"Cocoa Nuts," Alex pirouetted gleefully. "I forgot I told you all about it. Let's go," she said, hooking her hand through his arm. She flashed a parting smile at Leah.

But Andrei didn't move. "Leah, you come, too. You are skinny enough for me—a little ice cream won't hurt." Andrei's smile was warm and inviting, and Leah's heart skipped a beat.

"Leah has so much to do tonight. She must study for an exam tomorrow and rest up for all those rehearsals with you. We were just talking about that, Leah, weren't we?" Alex was smiling, but her eyes were narrowed and Leah got the message.

"Uh—that's right," Leah said. She shrugged her shoulders and stuffed her hands into the back pockets of her painter's pants. "I can't go tonight. Maybe some other time," she said weakly, giving them a little wave as they walked out the door.

The fact that Andrei looked disappointed did little to cheer her up. "Oh, Alex," Leah murmured under her breath. "What's gotten into you?" Alex might be ready to live with the fact that Leah got the prize part in the gala, but she was not about to share one moment of her precious time with Andrei. Leah didn't know what more she could do or say to convince Alex that she wasn't going to steal her guy—no matter how attractive she was beginning to find him.

Chapter 8

A week went by Leah in a blur, one rehearsal session with Andrei running into another. Having a ballet actually choreographed on her was certainly an honor. But Leah was paying a price for being the chosen one. By the next week, her exhilaration had given way to exhaustion. And she woke up Thursday morning from a dream she'd been having repeatedly for days now. One she couldn't quite forget but was too scared to remember.

It was the kind of dream she always had when she was working more intensely than usual at the school. Her body was so involved with the steps that even when she slept, she couldn't stop dancing. She'd wake up sweaty and hot in the middle of the night with her leg in a charley horse and the bunion on her right toe throbbing. But she'd be afraid to go to sleep again, fearing that the dream would repeat itself yet again. Andrei, of course, was part of it. The house lights would dim, and Leah would creep to the center of the stage. When the curtain went up, she'd always be surprised at the size of the Opera House. The huge auditorium gaped open like a mouth, and Leah had this terrible feeling that the dark was about to swallow her. A million pairs of eyes glowed from the audience.

Then the music would start. The first note would bring her legs to life. She'd take a first hesitant step toward the backdrop, which was a round, painted moon. Then she would feel herself pulled away into a series of low attitude turns and arabesques, always reaching for the moonlight, but running away from it at the same time. The spotlight, growing into a bigger and bigger circle, moved along the floorboards with her, until it merged with the spot which lit up Andrei. Leah would rush toward Andrei's outstretched arms, but in her dream she would pass right through them, as if he were a ghost, a figment of her imagination. She'd keep rushing forward, unable to stop, leaping into space right off the stage into the gaping darkness that a few moments before had been the backdrop. She kept flying through the air, unable to will herself to touch ground, and a voice from somewhere deep inside her would start to scream. Behind her back the audience would be chanting: "Third-rate. Third-rate. Third-rate." At the first words of the chant Leah would wake up, her legs cramped and her heart racing.

She hated the dream. Of course, Leah was used to bad dreams before performances. Even back home in San Lorenzo, before her teacher Hannah Greene's recitals, Leah had had terrible dreams. They were comprised of the usual fears—missing toe shoes; forgetting her steps; coming out to dance *Swan Lake* in a shaggy-dog costume. But none were ever this frightening.

"Leah, you aren't concentrating," Andrei said later that afternoon. The Matinee was just two days away, and Leah had totally blanked out on the choreography. For the first time since they started working together, he actually yelled at her. Leah knew she deserved it. They had worked on the same passage of the dance for half an hour, and every time they ran through it, Leah got worse.

Leah looked down at her feet and rubbed her bare arm across her forehead. "I'm hot. I'm tired and—and—" The accusation Leah had held back all week burst forth. She couldn't keep it back anymore. She was too tired to care what Andrei decided to do about her now. "You don't want me to dance with you anyway."

"Leah, what do you mean by that?" said Andrei, taking a step toward her.

She hugged her arms to herself, turning so he couldn't see her face. "You never wanted me to do this—Alex was your first choice. But you needed an American girl, so you picked Pam. She couldn't dance, and so you settled for me. I'm not good enough to be dancing with you, and that's that. I don't want to dance it anymore. I don't want to dance with you anymore." Leah was shouting. Her bottom lip trembled, and she didn't care if Andrei saw her cry.

Andrei's reaction surprised her. He didn't try to touch her or come closer. "You are right. I did choose Pam first because Alex was not permitted to dance with me."

Leah squeezed her eyes shut tight and put her

hands over her ears. Hearing the truth from Andrei's lips made everything that much worse. But she could not block out his voice, so she dropped her arms limply to her side.

"I chose you last because you were not the girl I had in mind. But, Leah, I like to dance with you. You must understand that I am happy Pam cannot do this with me, because I think it is turning out better with you as my partner."

Leah heard him approaching her and braced herself in case he touched her.

"And I feel just like you do," he said softly.

Leah whirled around, her blue eyes flashing. "You don't know how I feel. You couldn't possibly," she cried, turning her back to him.

Andrei didn't seem to understand her. He shrugged. "Just like you, I do not feel like dancing one more step of this. I am sick of it. I have never been so bored. It is my own ballet, and it puts me to sleep. I hate it."

In spite of herself Leah grew curious.

"Do you know why?" Andrei asked.

Leah shook her head slowly. He put his hands on her shoulders and forced her to face him. She hung her head, refusing to meet his eyes.

Without missing a beat Andrei continued. "Because we are almost perfect."

Leah's head snapped up sharply. She just had to laugh. "Sure, absolutely perfect," she said sarcastically. Then she found herself looking into his eyes, and she felt as though she were about to drown in their blue depths. For the tenth time that week her heart began beating a little faster. She deliberately stepped out of Andrei's reach and averted her glance. She didn't like the way he was making her feel. He belonged to Alex. He had no right to have such blue, bewitching eyes. Just being next to him these days drove every thought out of her head. No wonder she couldn't dance right. When she was with him, she was finding it impossible to think about dance.

"Leah, you do not have experience with this," Andrei said gently. "When you create a new ballet, it seems as if things will never come together. It feels the worst just before it gets better. You are making this ballet better than I ever dreamed it could be. Trust me." He ran his finger down her arm and took her hand.

Leah's legs felt all wobbly. "What else can I do?" she asked softly. She let go of Andrei's hand and walked over to the rosin box. With firm deliberate movements she ground the toes of her shoes into the sticky substance. For a moment she wondered if she was crazy, trying to be a dancer. Would she have to go through all this doubt, pain, and hurt, not to mention the bad dreams, before every performance? Was it part of the game to have these crazy, conflicting feelings about her partners—especially her really attractive partners? Leah stole a glance upward at Andrei, who, as he talked, rested his hand on her arm. Why did he have to be such a touchy-feely sort of person? Leah wondered. Her biggest problem now was remembering the choreography to *Circles*, but instead all she could think about was Andrei.

Leah forced her eyes away from the mirror and took a couple of deep breaths, trying to still her racing heart. Was this just a crush, or was it love? What was this funny feeling inside her every time he looked her in the eye, or touched her, or

smiled? It was very hard to dance with an adorable guy day after day and not begin to feel
something. Leah wished with all her heart there
were someone she could talk to, some other
dancer, someone she could trust who was older
and more experienced. She was beginning to wonder what was wrong with her. First James, and
now Andrei. Andrei was not as dashing as James,
but he was so much kinder and more compas-
sionate. No wonder she felt drawn to him. But
even if the feeling were mutual, what could Leah
do? Alex had fallen in love with Andrei first. And
Alex was her best friend.

If only I could quit—walk out of here and never
come back. The thought surfaced in her mind like
a fragile bubble, the kind you blow when you are
very little and want to touch before it pops. Leah
was entranced by it, but only for a moment. She
was born to dance, and nothing—not her stub-
born feet, her addled brain, and certainly not
Andrei's blue eyes—was going to stop her now.
When she turned around again, she was ready to
work.

Andrei motioned the accompanist to start where
they had left off. With a newfound firmness Leah
spoke up, "Andrei, can we take it from the top?"

"From the very beginning?"

Leah nodded. Andrei stared at her a moment
and then agreed.

The haunting music started again, and this time
Leah's dancing was inspired.

In the beginning of the dance they moved in
large circles, at times almost touching each other,
and then suddenly spiraling away. All at once the
steps became clear to Leah—the feeling, the move-

ment, and the shape of the whole ballet. Andrei told her to imagine how she would feel if she learned that there was life somewhere out in space. Leah's movements grew increasingly expansive. She jumped into the first lift, while Andrei, his hand on her rib cage, raised her high above his head. She gazed into his eyes, never wanting to stop looking at him. During the middle section of the ballet they never stopped touching one another. It was as if Andrei was causing her to "feel" the dance through his touch. She sensed he was conveying to her what he wanted her to do. For the first time while dancing the piece, Leah felt the role with her whole body. She didn't want to go far from Andrei or let go of his hand, but some force was pulling her. It was as strong as what was pulling him off toward the wings, in spiraling circles. Leah's movements matched his, and she ended up across the studio floor from Andrei as the music began to fade.

The last notes died away, and Andrei was instantly at Leah's side. "That was so beautiful. I felt it here." He thumped his chest a couple of times. "Leah, I love the way you dance. You move with so much feeling." With that he scooped her in his arms and spun her around and kissed her right on her smiling lips.

Andrei finally set her down by the dressing room and Leah gasped to find herself face to face with Kay. The petite girl was standing in the doorway. From the look on her face, Leah knew she had seen everything.

"Uh—hi!" Leah said, blushing furiously. She could just kill herself—whatever had possessed her to tell Kay to meet her here? And where was

Alex? The three girls had planned to go out together after Leah's rehearsal. She stared past Kay
and breathed a sigh of relief. Alex was nowhere in
sight.

Kay's surprised expression gave way to a wicked
grin. "See you in the dressing room," she said, as
she tiptoed out of the studio with exaggerated
care and closed the door behind her. Leah cringed.
Sometimes Kay was so obvious. Leah looked over
her shoulder at Andrei, but he didn't seem to
have noticed Kay at all. He was pacing the floor,
lost in thought, marking steps.

"See you later!" Leah said softly. But Andrei
didn't hear her, and following Kay's example, Leah
tiptoed out of the room.

Two minutes later, Leah was face-to-face with
her friend, racking her brain for some explanation. True to form, Kay wasn't about to give her a
chance. "Don't deny it—I saw it. He kissed you on
the mouth!" Kay's smile grew even wider.

"I'm not going to deny it," Leah said with dignity. She threw a shawl over her shoulders and
fished in her dance bag for a clean pair of socks.
"He *did* kiss me. He was happy because I finally
got the stupid ballet right." Leah tried to sound
businesslike, but her heart was still pounding. As
she bent over to untie the ribbons on her shoes,
again she let her fingers drift up to her lips and
vowed she'd never wash the spot again where he'd
kissed.

"I'm only glad Alex wasn't there to see it!" Kay
continued. She sat down on the floor and drew
her knees up to her chest. Leah had the uncomfortable feeling that she was about to become the
hottest item on Kay's grapevine.

Almost afraid to ask, Leah said, "Where—where is Alex?"

"Home. She's waiting to see if Andrei will call." Kay's large blue eyes narrowed as she watched Leah carefully. "Of course, in my humble opinion, I think she shouldn't bother. I've thought that all along. I've put my money on you."

"You've what?" Leah cried. "What money? What are you talking about?"

Kay grabbed a brush and began fussing with her hair. As she yanked the bristles through her thick black curls, she launched breezily into an explanation. "I told Katrina and Melanie that I thought Alex should stop mooning over our dear Mr. Levintoff as early as last week. It's quite obvious he prefers you."

Leah stared at Kay speechless, but her heart leapt at Kay's words.

"Everyone is taking sides. There's the Alex faction: Let's see, that's Suzanne, Linda, Kristin Nordstrom, and Sara Macey." Kay screwed up her expressive face in a pensive frown. "I think that's all. I'm on your side," she concluded brightly.

Leah clapped her hands over her ears. "Katherine Larkin, I don't want to hear one more word of this. What are you talking about? Alex is *dating* Andrei. Besides, I'm not at all interested in him." Leah got up and flounced over to the clothing rack.

While she dressed, she kept her back carefully turned away from Kay. What Kay was saying thrilled her, but at the same time it made her uneasy. Leah had no right to have these feelings toward Andrei, even if he was her partner, and even if he did kiss her. She had been dead serious when she told Alex she would never steal a guy from a friend. Still, Kay's words had sent her spirit soaring. No matter how she felt about Andrei inside, she was not going to betray Alex's trust.

"You know, Leah," Kay said softly. "I understand how you feel about Alex. But she hasn't been *dating* him really."

"Kay Larkin! They go out together all the time, and you know it!"

"Going to Cocoa Nuts or out for breakfast or lunch is one thing. But I don't think Andrei likes Alex that way. In fact, I am sure of it. And I could see by the way he was looking at you now when you danced with him, that you, not Alex, are the girl of his dreams."

Leah permitted herself a small sigh, then shook her head hard. She would not allow herself to listen to Kay's gossip.

Kay's next words sent a shock wave through her. "Alex doesn't own him, you know. They aren't married. He has a right to like who he wants. Just like he picked who he wanted for his ballet."

Leah's firm resolve was wavering. "Alex would feel just terrible . . ."

"Only for a little while," Kay said practically. "Besides, I know someone else will come along for her. She is so beautiful and exotic. What guy wouldn't fall for Alex? The trouble is, like most of us, she never gets a chance to meet anyone." Kay cut herself off and shook her head. "But that's not the point. It was all spelled out clear as day in Alex's tea leaves."

"You mean about meeting Andrei and his changing her life," Leah scoffed. "I don't believe all that."

"Well, you should," Kay pronounced solemnly. "If I remember correctly, he said 'Someone in this house will fall in love soon and a stranger will come here and change her life.'"

Leah blinked. That tea-leaves reading seemed so long ago. She had forgotten the specifics of Andrei's prediction.

"So, Leah, it is obvious that the 'someone' in our house wasn't Alex, but you."

"Kay," Leah warned.

Kay charged on with her explanation. "And Andrei, just like I said that first night, is no stranger to Alex. He's an old friend. But he *was* a stranger to you." Kay reached over and shook Leah's shoulders. "You know, I think you don't *want* to see, but I suspect you really do believe those tea leaves. Andrei was destined not for Alex but for you, Leah Stephenson!"

Leah balled up her tights and tossed them at Kay. "Will you be quiet, Larkin. You and your dumb superstitions." Leah checked her watch and jumped up. "And while you're playing matchmaker, we are about to be late for a great film! Now we'll have to rush!" Leah, who usually hated rushing anywhere, was glad they'd have to make a mad dash for the movie theater. Now there'd be no time to waste talking about Andrei. Or thinking about that tea-leaves reading. Leah only wished there were some way to make the thrill in her heart go away when she heard Kay repeat Andrei's forecast.

In two seconds flat Leah was in her overalls and out the dressing room door, Kay trotting by her side. They turned the corner and bumped right into Andrei.

He smiled at Kay, then said to Leah, "We worked hard today, no?"

"Uh—yes." Leah suddenly felt terribly self-conscious. She had this crazy feeling he would kiss her again, right there in the third-floor hall of SFBA. She hung behind a little, so he'd walk downstairs next to Kay. When she finally felt brave enough to meet his eyes, she found he was looking out the window on top of the stairs, gazing at the rain.

"Where are you going?" he asked, sauntering slowly down the steps.

"Well, if we hurry we might just make it on time for the next show at the Redwood Cinema," Kay replied.

Andrei's face lit up. "You go to the movies? Now? Can I come?"

Leah began to say no, but Kay spoke up faster. "Wow, that would be great. I'm sure you'd like the film." She looked back up the stairs at Leah and let out a merry laugh before facing Andrei again. "It's about a Russian dancer. Baryshnikov is in it! It's called *The Turning Point*."

"I know of it!" Andrei said excitedly as they reached the ground floor.

"You've seen it already," Leah said hopefully. Just talking about Andrei with Kay had left her stomach in knots. Sitting next to him during a movie didn't promise to be good for Leah's turbulent state of mind.

"No, I have not. I want to very much." With that, Andrei took Leah's arm and guided her toward a sporty red Trans Am. Leah's eyebrows shot up. Kay whistled approvingly.

"Is this yours?" Kay ran her fingers down the

sleek finish as Leah tried to maneuver herself away from Andrei.

"I do not own it. The company helped me—I forget the word—lease it, for the time I work here. I pay for it, though." He made a face. "Cars are expensive to have here."

"But handy," Kay commented practically. "Now we won't be late."

Going to the movies with Andrei was definitely a mistake. She sat on one side of him, Kay on the other. Andrei held the popcorn, and every time she took some, her hand grazed his, and sparks of electricity went right up her arm.

Ten minutes into the film Leah wondered what had possessed her to see this movie again, though the answer really was simple. It could be summed up in a single word—Baryshnikov. Leah, like every other girl who studied ballet, had an all-consuming crush on the great Russian dancer. Dreams of someday being partnered by him had seen her through many a difficult moment in class. Now that Leah was at SFBA, she didn't have much time to moon over famous dancers. She'd even gotten to take class with one or two of her other idols, Lynne Vreeland for example, and just last week she had actually had dinner with Dimitri Sorokin. They had turned out to be real flesh-and-blood people, so Leah wasn't quite as susceptible to stars these days. Now that her heros and heroines were within reach, Leah found herself admiring them for their professionalism and technique and dreaming of them less. That's why she watched the movie as if seeing it for the first time. Before, she had only waited for the dancing parts, and like any other aspiring ballet dancer, had been lost in the subplot of the young girl who gets to dance with the famous hero of the film, Baryshnikov's soulful Yuri. But she hadn't paid much attention to the emotional plight of the characters.

Now she sat in the dark theater and just wanted to die. On-screen the movie's hero was singing a tear-jerking Russian folk tune to the accompaniment of a mellow guitar, and at that moment Baryshnikov the star was the farthest person from Leah's mind. The story of the Russian émigré dancer suddenly cut Leah to the quick. Poor Andrei, she thought. How homesick watching all this must make him!

As if he could hear her very thoughts, Andrei suddenly grabbed her hand. Keeping his eyes on the screen, he leaned closer to Leah. "I sometimes feel very alone, just like that." And for the briefest of moments he pillowed his head on Leah's shoulder. She reached up and tentatively stroked his thick, wavy hair. He looked at her, and his eyes glistened in the dark with tears. Leah leaned her face in toward his, and their lips were very close. Then Andrei straightened up and focused his attention back on the screen, holding her hand tightly until the credits rolled and the houselights went up.

Andrei parked the Trans Am right in front of Mrs. Hanson's, then opened the door for the girls. Leah and Kay scrambled out and ran through the rain up the steps to the boardinghouse. Andrei followed on their heels. They stood on the porch looking out at the deluge, trying to catch their breath. The rain and the fact they were soaked to the skin struck them as being funny, and the three of them broke into uncontrollable laughter.

Leah was still giggling when they entered the house.

"So how was the movie?" Alex's voice preceded her into the hall. She had her nose in a book and an apple in her hand.

"Great!" Kay managed to say before Alex looked up. Leah was sure she'd never forget the expression on Alex's face at that moment. Her astonished eyes went from Kay, to Andrei, to Leah. Her gaze finally rested on Leah, who stepped a little closer to Andrei, as if he could somehow protect her. He gave her hand a quick squeeze.

He walked right over to Alex, leaving a trail of puddles on the polished wood floor. "Hi, little one. Can I have a bite?" He gave her braid a friendly tug, then deftly stole the rosy apple from her hand. He tossed it in the air, so high it grazed the hall ceiling, then he caught it between his teeth. After a hearty chomp he pulled it out of his mouth. "I wanted first to be a clown in the circus, before I learned I could dance." He flashed an irresistibly boyish grin at Leah, winked at Kay, then handed Alex back what was left of her apple, causing the color in her cheeks to rise.

Andrei hung his soggy jacket on an empty hook on the coat rack, then sauntered past Alex through the arched entrance to the living room. He flopped down in a chair, dangling one leg over the arm. Hooking his thumbs in his bright-blue suspenders, he began imitating Baryshnikov's deeper voice. Then he laughed, straightening up in his seat. "I wish you had been there. I missed you." His blue eyes innocently searched Alex's dark ones. "Did you have a date tonight?"

"Did I—" Alex started, then cut herself off. The antique Bavarian cuckoo clock that hung over the bookcase began to chime.

Kay looked from Leah to Alex and said in a falsely bright voice, "Well, I don't know about you two, but I've got a pile of homework to do. Good night, Andrei, I had fun!" She turned on her heels and raced up the stairs. Leah frantically tried to figure out how to make a graceful exit and follow her, but Andrei wasn't about to give her a chance.

He sprang up from the chair, stretching his arms. "I have work to do, too. On our dance. I thought of a good name for our dance. Tell Alex what it is, Leah."

Leah tried to swallow. Her throat was tight, and her mouth had gone all dry. *"Circles."* She spoke so low Alex actually leaned forward to catch it. *"Circles,"* Leah repeated a second time, her voice sounding loud and hollow.

Alex didn't say a word, did not even bother to look at Leah. She kept her eyes on Andrei, and Leah was glad she couldn't see Alex's face. Andrei grabbed his jacket and turned to leave. He reached over to Alex and affectionately tousled her hair.

Leah was still standing in the hall. She clutched her wet sweater jacket in her hands and wondered what to do. Andrei started for the door. He got as far as the table, then turned around, a quizzical expression on his broad face. "Leah, it was nice going to the movies with you." Then he backtracked and bent down over Leah to kiss her. It was only a peck on the cheek, and a quick one at that. But he had kissed her right in front of Alex. Leah closed her eyes and wanted to cry.

The front door slammed shut, and Leah came to her senses. Her eyes snapped open. "Alex—" Without thinking, she started toward her friend. There had to be a way to make this all better, to take away the awful pain that was beginning to show on Alex's face. "It's not what—" Leah broke off and dropped her gaze to the floor. How could she lie like that? It was exactly what Alex thought. The truth was that Leah had liked Andrei kissing her, now and earlier in the studio. Remembering the way he had looked at her during the movie and how close he had been to kissing her then, Leah knew there was no turning back now. She had allowed herself to fall in love with Andrei regardless of Alex's feelings.

"I don't have anything to say to you," Alex said, her throaty voice strained and tight. "I should have known that around this place there was no such thing as a real friend." A sob choked off whatever else Alex was about to say. Tears streamed down her face, and she stood there staring helplessly at Leah. Then suddenly she turned and bolted up the stairs.

"Oh, Alex," Leah cried after her. She started up the steps, taking them two at a time. But on the small landing, halfway up to the second floor, Leah stopped. She hugged her arms to herself and leaned back against the windowsill. Every instinct prompted her to run to Alex, to say she was sorry, to say she hadn't meant things with Andrei to go this far. It was clear to Leah tonight how much Andrei cared for her, needed her— maybe even really loved her. All along, Andrei had treated Alex as a friend, a close, much-loved friend—but still just a friend. Leah saw that now. It was just as she had suspected from the start.

Leah straightened her shoulders and proceeded more slowly up the stairs. Alex was hurting, and Leah would do anything to make her friend's pain disappear. But she wouldn't lie, and she couldn't pretend she wasn't in love with Andrei. And she hadn't flirted with him or anything like that. As Kay had said, Alex didn't own the young Russian dancer. He was free to love whom he pleased. Suddenly, Andrei's reading didn't seem so superstitious at all, Leah thought, trailing her finger along the ridge of the polished wooden banister. He had glimpsed the future—*their* future. He just hadn't predicted it clearly enough to prevent all this trouble between Leah and Alex, and this upset Leah. Still, as Kay had said, in time Alex would get over it. For a moment Leah tried to picture her future years at SFBA without Alex as her friend. It was a terribly empty future and not very much fun. Alex had to get over it. She just had to.

Chapter 9

If only Diana were a better friend—
someone she could talk to, Leah thought ruefully
Friday afternoon. She sat in the North Beach Café
across from the Bay Area Ballet dancer, wishing
Diana Chen were a person she could trust. What
she needed right now was someone to talk to,
another dancer more experienced and just a little
bit older than herself. Leah peered up at Diana
through her long eyelashes.

Diana looked friendly today, more approach-
able than usual, in what she had called her knock-
about weekend outfit. She wore a cream silk shirt
with a floppy bow around the neck, trim wheat-
colored pants, and tiny gold hoops in her ears.
When they met in the SFBA office after Leah's
morning class, Leah had felt downright dowdy in
her denim miniskirt and purple cowboy boots.

Diana's whirlwind tour of second-hand shops
and trendy, inexpensive boutiques had helped Leah
find the perfect dress for the party after tomorrow's Matinee. But it didn't make Leah feel any
better. All the clothes in the world couldn't hide

the way she felt about herself today. Deep down inside she was convinced she'd become a terrible person. After last night what girl would want to be her friend? Not after what she had done to Alex. Leah let out a sad sigh and absently twiddled the fringes hanging from her cowboy shirt.

Diana cleared her throat. In a light, playful voice she said, "Don't let those pregala blues get you down!" She paused, but when Leah didn't even look up, Diana went on, sounding earnest this time. "If you don't eat, you're going to get, number one, too skinny, and number two, weak. You'll be rehearsing late tonight and won't have a chance for dinner. You haven't even touched your salad." There was a new, almost maternal, tone in Diana's voice, and Leah slowly looked up; her sad blue eyes studied Diana's face. Her concern looked so genuine that for a moment Leah was tempted to tell her everything.

Diana leaned forward on her elbows and twisted the delicate bracelet she wore around her wrist. "Or is it more than nerves?" Diana suggested, leaning back in her seat and scrutinizing Leah.

"What makes you say that?" Leah burst out suddenly, feeling very defensive. She hadn't thought her problems with Alex and Andrei were public knowledge. Kay had told her this morning she wouldn't breathe a word of what happened last night to a soul. And though gossip came as natural to her as breathing, Kay never made promises she couldn't keep.

"Because not so long ago I was fifteen, too. I also danced in the gala my first year at school—of course, not with anyone quite as distinguished as

Andrei Levintoff." She stressed Andrei's name slightly—or was Leah just imagining things?

Leah tried to lure Diana off the subject. "What did you dance?" Leah asked.

"Does it matter?" Diana asked quietly. She paused to sip some water, and set the glass down on the small circular table. With her finger she traced the flowered pattern of the wrought iron surface. "It's Andrei, Leah, isn't it?"

Leah answered a little too quickly. "No. No. Andrei has nothing to do with it."

Diana motioned for the waiter. He refilled her coffee and took away the basket of rolls, leaving Leah's salad. She still hadn't eaten a bite.

Diana sipped her coffee and looked out the window. Leah realized Diana was going to let the matter of Andrei drop. She was almost sure of it.

"As for James—" Diana's face took Leah off guard. She must have looked startled, because Diana looked at her and began to laugh. "I would like to apologize again. It was just that I thought he would be my partner. I made a mistake there—I let concern about my own future get in the way of my teaching. I've talked to Madame about that, and I don't want to teach as much this season. Of course, as it turns out, I won't get much of a chance."

"I heard you'll be opening in *Giselle* in January," Leah remarked.

"Yes, and there will be other things for me coming up, and I'll be busy with rehearsals."

Leah just nodded. She was more comfortable with Diana than she thought she'd be, though she had a feeling the ballerina was holding something back.

"I wanted to tell you that before I asked you more about Andrei."

Leah's head snapped up. "But—"

Diana wasn't about to let Leah object. She went on quickly. "Now, Leah, he is a very attractive young man and an electrifying dancer. Appearing with him Saturday in the Matinee is a wonderful boost for your career. And I think he's a good person, too. Everyone in the company likes him. His ego doesn't get in the way of relating to other people. That's rare in a dancer of his stature. But, Leah—" Diana paused and held Leah's glance—"be careful!"

"Of what?" Leah asked a little too shrilly. The memory of Andrei's kiss sent a pleasant little shiver through her.

Diana smiled. It was a motherly or sisterly kind of smile and put Leah on guard. "Of getting involved with him."

"I'm not involved with him!" Leah cried. "What— or who—gave you that idea?" Leah shrank back in her chair. "No, don't bother to tell me—it was Pam, wasn't it?" Two red spots bloomed on Leah's cheeks and beneath the table, she twisted her napkin in her hand.

Diana looked genuinely confused. "What's this got to do with Pam?"

"Everything. You like Pam. She confides in you. She's livid that she got hurt and that Andrei picked me as his partner. She is your favorite dancer around here," Leah said angrily. "Don't try to deny it."

"I won't." Diana was still smiling, but she had a

hard look in her eyes. "And I have a right to prefer one student's style above another's. Just like Andrei."

Leah cringed. They were back to Andrei again, and suddenly she felt cornered. It seemed perfectly obvious to Leah now. Pam had blabbed to Diana about Andrei and her holding hands on the veranda. For some reason Diana was jealous of her. The way she had been jealous of her and James.

"He's going to be *your* partner!" Leah stated rather than asked. She sat very erect in her chair, and her voice was cold, accusing. "Isn't he? That's why you want me to stay away from him. You're afraid—just like you were with James, that he'll like dancing with me better than with you."

Diana threw her hands up in the air. "Leah Stephenson, you are just too much. I am not jealous of you. Why should I be?" There was a slightly condescending note in Diana's voice that made Leah very happy she hadn't chosen to confide in her. "Yes, I am going to be dancing the *Giselle* with Andrei. He'll be my main partner this season, but he'll partner—" Diana bit her lip and cut herself off. She smoothed her already tidy black hair back toward her bun. "He'll partner other people, too."

Leah met Diana's level gaze and waited a beat before speaking her piece. "Like me, someday?"

Diana clenched her fist and cursed slightly under her breath. "Okay, I deserved that. Because of James." She spoke in a tight, staccato voice. "But, Leah—" Diana's harsh expression softened and Leah couldn't ignore the plea in Diana's voice— "be careful of Andrei. Things get confused sometimes when your partner is handsome, so gifted, and has so much charisma. It gets hard to distinguish between what happens in the studio or onstage, and real life."

Leah looked down at her hands, a little embarrassed she had reacted to Diana so strongly. Some instinct told her Diana meant well. And for a fleeting instant her warning about Andrei somehow rang true, though Leah had no idea why.

But being partnered by Andrei was something every young ballet dancer would envy. Diana herself had termed Leah's role in the Saturday Matinee 'a real plum.' And Leah would always be a threat, particularly to Diana, especially when she was a professional dancer in a year or two. They were not only the same body type and size, but they seemed suited for the same roles. No, Leah couldn't afford to listen to Diana's advice, certainly not where Andrei was concerned. Leah knew firsthand how devious another dancer could be if she felt threatened. Pam had taught her that, and Diana, too, and Leah wasn't about to get burned twice by the same fire.

"Kay's new ballet should have been called *Hair*," Melanie Carlucci quipped twenty minutes before curtain time on Saturday.

Leah looked up from her spot at the long dressing table and, in spite of the butterflies in her stomach, laughed. "I can't believe she actually cut it because of how she wanted to look on stage during her own ballet. It will take years to grow back." Leah sighed, remembering Kay's thick mop of almost-black curls. Her friend had chopped it all off this morning, and was left with a head full of ringlets that made her look prettier than ever, but not at all like a ballet dancer. "She does look great, though," she commented aloud.

"But what will Madame say?" Suzanne wondered in a hushed voice. "No one else in the school has short hair—not as short as that?"

"It's all anyone can talk about!" Melanie remarked, then stood up and presented her back to Linda. "Powder me, please." Linda obliged with generous pats of the powder puff, and Melanie craned her neck to see the effect in the mirror. The freckles on her skin hardly showed now. But the cloud of talcum settling around her made her sneeze. "Thank God this tutu is white."

Melanie was standing right in front of Alex, but Alex didn't seem to notice she was there. "Hey, Sorokin, want me to do yours?"

Alex just nodded. As Melanie attended to Alex's shoulders and back, Leah caught Alex's glance in the mirror and quickly turned away. She got up from the low stool and walked over to the costume rack. Frieda Heinz, the girls' dresser, helped Leah into a filmy pink dance skirt. She held Leah at arm's length and frowned at the sagging waistline. "You'd better not lose any more weight," Frieda warned, picking up the glasses that hung from a string around her neck. She settled them on her nose and whipped an already threaded needle out of the pincushion she wore on her wrist.

As she tucked in the excess fabric, Leah tried to make light of her lack of appetite. She was so thin these days that dropping even a couple of pounds definitely wasn't good for her. She made a resolution to indulge in some ice cream at the party tonight, and said apologetically to Frieda, "I guess I couldn't eat because of nerves." Saying that, Leah felt Alex's eyes on her back but willed herself not to turn around. That Alex was hurt about Andrei was understandable, but Leah couldn't let Alex's pain interfere with her concentration. After the performance I can try to get through to her, she thought.

Frieda knotted the thread and patted Leah's slim hips. "There, that's better now!" She eyed her handiwork then took off her glasses. "This costume suits your coloring. Dance well, Leah." She gave Leah's shoulders a parting squeeze and turned to help another girl dress.

Leah smoothed the delicately patterned fabric of her skirt over her matching leotard. The transparent pink material was pale and printed with overlapping large circles of blue and violet. Before Leah had come to SFBA, she would have been envious of the girls wearing traditional tutus, but she had quickly learned to love the feel of a more natural skirt, the way the breeze from the wings of the stage lifted it, blowing it out from her legs or sometimes making it cling. Wearing this costume, she didn't feel like a dancer so much as a girl who was dancing because she was in love. It really did make her feel like flying, right into Andrei's arms.

"Five minutes till curtain!" The announcement echoed throughout the backstage area of the Opera House. Leah's throat went dry.

The second act of *La Bayadère* was first on the program: Alex, Melanie, and Abby had solo parts in it. The lead was Diana Chen, who was being partnered by Don. Next was a short expressionistic, much-acclaimed ballet, with sets that looked like prehistoric cave paintings, that was choreographed by Johnny Cullum, Kay's choreography teacher. Kay's ballet, which was still a mystery, followed. And last of all was *Circles*. Leah wished she didn't have to wait until the end, well aware that dancing last—with Andrei—was the place of honor on the program. And that critics would leave the theater with the last ballet performed freshest in their minds. Knowing she was on display as one of the "new baby ballerinas" that the SFBA press office had lauded nearly frightened her to death. Her nerves weren't up to waiting, not that waiting for anything had ever been Leah Stephenson's strong point.

So she was surprised at how fast the time flew.

The first strains of music to *La Bayadère* seemed to have just started when Leah suddenly realized that Kay was halfway through her ballet. Along with the other students, Leah watched spellbound from the wings. For ten whole minutes she forgot about Andrei, Alex, Diana Chen, and her own stage fright. Kay's ballet was that good. It was called *Sounds*, and Kay had been telling the truth when she said there was no music for this dance. Katrina, Linda, Kenny, and Kay moved only to the noises, sounds, and whisperings of bird calls, rainfall, and the whistle of wind through a Rocky Mountain canyon. Leah knew Kay had been intrigued by the school library's collection of nature tapes, primarily used for stress reduction and relaxation. But only Kay had seen them as accompaniment for a dance. *Sounds* was full of trick moves, quirky changes of direction, and to Leah's eye, seemed fiendishly hard to dance. It was the kind of ballet that demanded you move in time to the count of beats in your head. There was no melody to carry you along. And yet the piece was charged with emotion. The four performers wore full-body leotards hand-painted with shadowy designs that resembled wild animals. Leah watched and understood why Kay had grown tired lately, dancing "the same old sweet things." Here was a side of Kay Leah had never seen before. No one outside of choreography class had. Her steps were full of whimsy, humor, and a kind of sharp wit, and at the same time they made Leah a little sad. "That little one is made to make great dances," Andrei whispered in Leah's ear as the four young dancers sped through the final combination.

Leah jumped. She hadn't known he was anywhere nearby.

"Hey, don't be nervous." Andrei tossed aside the towel he was holding and slung his arm over Leah's shoulder. His touch sent a delightful shudder down her spine. She marveled at how safe she felt with Andrei as she leaned against him. Then she spotted Alex looking directly at them, her large dark eyes filled with tears. As the curtain crashed down, Alex turned abruptly and headed down the hallway toward the dressing room. Leah wanted to follow, but she needed to tell Kay how great she was and then warm up for her own performance.

She barely finished her stretches, and then it was time.

"We're on!" Andrei peeled off his leg warmers and squeezed her hand.

"Good luck," Kay whispered from the wings.

Behind her Leah could see that Alex was back. Alex seemed to look right through Leah, but the fact that she was bothering to watch *Circles* at all gave Leah hope for their friendship. She scurried into the opposite wing. From in front of the curtain she heard the opening bars of the Debussy score. Then the curtain lifted. For a moment Leah couldn't remember her entrance. She began to panic. Her hands fluttered to her hair. It hung loose for this ballet, and she nervously combed her fingers through the carefully arranged waves.

The stage was in total darkness. A dim circle of light appeared, and Andrei stepped into it. Then Leah counted to six and glided onstage. There was no scenery to speak of, only the dark night of the backdrop, painted with pale stars and the big round moon. After the first few steps Leah's mind stopped racing and her body took over. Now she understood the reason for the hours and hours of practice. It wasn't just to learn and perfect the steps, but to get them in her bloodstream. Once her initial stage fright passed, Leah found the music sweeping her across the stage, into Andrei's arms and away again. The first touch of his fingers lit a fire in Leah, and she stopped dancing steps and began revealing her feelings in the best way she knew how—not with words, not with thoughts, but through every gesture of her well-trained body.

It seemed their dance had just begun when it was over. The music stopped, the spotlights dimmed, and Leah and Andrei glided apart, into their separate wings. Leah stood dazed a moment, still lost in the wonder of their dance. Then someone was shaking her, and people were shouting.

"That was so beautiful, Leah, so very beautiful," Kay cried, wiping the tears from her face.

"Curtain calls!" Leah felt herself being steered back on stage. Andrei was suddenly by her side, his hand on her waist. From the half-blank look on his face, she could tell he felt the same way she did—still locked with her in the dance, two lonely people touching for a short time.

The curtain went up, and the applause was deafening. To Leah's amazement, flowers rained down from the balconies. Andrei gallantly scooped up an armful and presented them to her. Leah forgot to bow and just faced the audience, her smile radiant. Then Andrei took her hand again, and she remembered proper ballet protocol. He bowed with one hand over his heart, and she sank into a deep curtsy. Then he helped her up, and the curtain went down. The curtain went up again, and she and Andrei stepped forward into the applause. As they rose from their bow, a tuxedoed man marched out of the wings and presented Leah with the biggest bouquet of flowers she'd ever seen.

"From me," Andrei whispered under his breath, and she sank into another bow. His hand around her waist steadied her as she gracefully straightened up. On impulse, Leah plucked a large pink rose from the arrangement and handed it to Andrei. His eyebrows shot up, but his smile was brilliant, and the roar from the audience drowned out whatever it was he whispered as he bent over her hand and kissed it.

When the curtain closed for the last time, everyone rushed onstage to hug and kiss her and congratulate Andrei on his successful new ballet. The crowd parted slightly for Madame, and Leah curtsied prettily to her teacher. Madame inclined her head graciously, then gathered Leah in her arms. "That was wonderful, Leah. I knew you could do justice to this piece. We're very proud of you, all of us."

Madame's words made Leah's heart sing, and she hugged her teacher back. Then the smile froze on her face. Over Madame's shoulder she spotted Alex, who had changed from her tutu into a white dress that clung to her body. Her cheeks were as pale as her outfit, and she stood alone off-stage. She regarded Leah with hurt eyes and seemed oblivious to the tears coursing down her face. The heady, bubbly feeling inside of Leah's chest suddenly died. She disentangled herself from Madame and rushed past Andrei.

By the time she got through the crowd, Alex was gone.

Chapter 10

"*This is truly your party!*" Kay exclaimed as she and Leah inched their way through the crowd that hovered around the refreshment table. Every couple of steps they took, someone would congratulate Leah. Now and then somebody recognized Kay.

"Why, thank you," Leah said with a newfound graciousness, and managed to shake the hand of a diamond-bedecked woman who had just praised her performance. Then under her breath she commented to Kay, "It's your party, too, silly. Andrei's *Circles* is a wonderful ballet, but your *Sounds* is a masterpiece."

Melanie spoke up from the other side of Kay. "She's right, you know. That man there—with the pot belly—"

Kay interrupted, with a giggle. "He could use a year of classes with Madame. She'd get him into shape."

"That's beside the point," Melanie said, giving Kay a little shake. "He's the top critic for *Foot-*

Notes and he called *Sounds* the most brilliant thing he's ever seen."

Kay blushed with pride, but protested demurely, "You're making that up!"

"I am not. And he also said that Leah was the best dancer the school has produced in years."

"He did?" Leah shrieked. Several guests turned around and smiled at the three girls.

Leah couldn't remember when she had felt so embarrassed. Direct compliments unnerved her. It was easier to smile from the stage to a houseful of clapping strangers than to hear someone come right out and say she was good. She finally reached the table and handed cups of fruit punch back to her friends. She took a small sip from her own glass. She should have been hungry and thirsty, but there was a knot in her stomach that wouldn't go away. It had to do with Alex, who was nowhere in sight. Leah wondered if, somehow, she had slipped past Madame Preston and headed home.

"On second thought," Kay said, gulping down the sweet drink, "it's Andrei's bash. Would you look at that?" She nudged Leah's elbow. At first Leah couldn't see through the crowd. Tables filled the spacious interior lobby of the Opera House. Knots of people sauntered from the buffet, to the bar and back again, and it was hard to make out a single face in the packed room. At last, however, Leah spotted Andrei. His hair was slightly damp from the shower, and he had slicked it back, but where it was drying, it had already started to curl over the collar of his pale dress shirt. He had a drink in one hand and looked very comfortable being the center of attention. He was surrounded

by admirers. Leah would have called them group-
ies, but they were very rich and elegantly dressed,
and Leah knew that without their money the Bay
Area Ballet itself, as well as the school, would
cease to exist.

Andrei happened to glance across the room
and catch Leah's eye. He toasted her with his
glass, then broke out of the circle of fans and
made his way toward her.

"Leah," he called warmly, still some feet away.
"I was looking for you. I want you to meet these
people. Mr. Mooreland from the big dance magazine is here. He wants to do an interview with
you—if Madame agrees." He stopped talking and
looked her up and down. His blue eyes glowed
approval. "Your dress—what do you call the
color?—I like it. You look wonderful."

Leah glanced down in confusion. "Why—why
thank you," she stammered. Their performance
this afternoon seemed to have strengthened the
bond she felt between them. She looked up at
Andrei. "The color is rose. I picked it out because
it's like my costume," she explained, leaving out
the part about Diana. Matching her gala dress to
her costume had been Diana's idea, but Leah
wasn't in the mood to give her credit.

Before Leah could protest, Andrei had hooked
her arm through his and was steering her into the
middle of the crowd. Leah felt a tingle of excitement when she realized that people were staring
at the two of them with knowing smiles. They will
know I'm more than his partner! she thought. And
she held herself a little taller and walked as carefully across the floor as if it were a stage.

"Very nice, Leah, I must say!" Pam's drawl

stopped Leah cold. She looked first to the right, then the left, but the redhead was behind her.

Andrei saw her first. His smile widened, and he reached out and touched Pam's face. "You are better now? I hear you will be back in class next week."

"Why, yes," Pam answered, pleased but obviously surprised by Andrei's concern. "I am just sorry I had to miss today."

Andrei didn't reply directly to that. "As long as you dance again. You are a good dancer and will do well, I think." He started to move away from Pam, when she gave a little cry. That stopped him in his tracks.

"What is wrong?" He dropped Leah's hand and held out his arm to Pam. She clamped her arm around his forearm and leaned on him heavily.

"Oh," she cried, with a flutter of her dark lashes. "Nothing, I just put too much weight on my bad leg."

Leah tried not to look skeptical. Until Andrei turned to leave, Pam had seemed perfectly healthy, or at least not in pain. The only sign that she was injured was her outfit. Leah figured her knee was still taped. Pam had exchanged her usual miniskirted look for a pair of loose, flowing silk pants and a black halter top. One side of her thick hair was pinned back, and over her ear she had tucked a pale gardenia. The strong fragrance turned Leah's stomach.

Pam turned to Leah and sounded almost apologetic as she said, "Actually, I did just want to tell you, both of you, how well you danced."

Leah forced herself to murmur her thanks.

"And," Pam continued in a silky voice, "I wanted to be the first to congratulate you."

Leah's back stiffened. Pam would never, ever, congratulate her on anything. Then she realized Pam wasn't looking at her at all. The redhead's huge green eyes were turned up toward Andrei's unsuspecting face.

"Congratulate me?" Andrei looked puzzled.

"Well," Pam purred. "I do believe it is the proper thing to do—congratulate a man on his upcoming marriage!"

Andrei looked shocked, only for a moment. Then he threw back his head and laughed. "Yes, I am getting married. It was a secret. But it is no secret now!" He regarded Pam quizzically and asked, "How did you find out?"

Leah took a step backward. Andrei getting married? Pam had to be making all this up. She was trying to get at Leah because of the gala. Besides, Andrei hadn't mentioned anything about another girl. And neither had Alex. Unless this had something to do with Alex. Leah shivered. Alex was young to get married, but she'd be eighteen soon. Leah's pulse thundered in her ears. She barely took in Pam's next words.

"My daddy sent me a clipping from a New York paper. She's a dancer, I hear. Her name is Claire."

"Yes, Claire DuParc. We will dance here together after American Ballet Theatre's season at the Metropolitan Opera House in New York."

Suddenly half the room was swarming around the young Russian dancer congratulating him, asking questions, and giving Leah the blessed opportunity to slip away.

She forced herself to walk slowly until she left the main lobby, then she bolted down a set of stairs that led to the backstage entrance, her skirt fluttering behind her. She ran down the carpeted hallway and opened the door. She slipped into the silent corridor and closed the door behind her. Leaning her back against the cool metal surface, she slid down to the floor and stared blankly at the red safety light at the other end of the hall. Her mind was a jumble of disconnected words and phrases. Andrei. Married. Claire. "Claire," Leah whispered the name aloud. Where had she heard that name before? "Claire and Andrei. Andrei and Claire." She strung the two names together and hit the door hard with the palm of her hand. It sounded all wrong. Couldn't Andrei see that? It didn't sound at all as wonderful as Andrei and Leah. Leah suddenly moaned aloud. She had just remembered her journal. The other night she'd stayed up late covering two whole pages with their names. Andrei and Leah. She must have written it a hundred times. All at once she felt so humiliated. Why hadn't he told her? Why had he led her on? She hugged her arms to her chest and held herself tight. A strong pressure built up behind her eyes. She pounded the floor. Once. Twice. Three times. The third time she struck it so hard her hand stung. Reliving the moment of the awful revelation finally reduced Leah to tears. She covered her eyes with her hands and sobbed until she thought her chest would burst from the pain of it.

"Who is there?" a frightened voice spoke up from somewhere to the left of Leah.

Leah's head snapped up. She scrambled to her

feet, feeling defenseless and ashamed. Someone had heard her mumbling Andrei's name and crying. She put her hand on the doorknob and thought of getting out of there before someone recognized her. Then she noticed where she was. The corridor bent sharply to her left, leading to another set of stairs and the dressing rooms.

"Is someone there?" the voice asked again. This time Leah recognized it.

"Alex?" she cried, poking her head around the corner. Halfway up the stairs Alex sat huddled in a little ball. "Oh, Alex." Leah climbed quickly to her side.

Alex looked at her for a moment, then right through her. "Leave me alone," she said in a monotone.

Leah put her hands on her hips and stared down at her friend. "No. I will not leave you alone."

Alex's eyes narrowed. "Then I will leave you alone." She got up and dusted off the back of her skirt.

"See if I care," Leah said. She hurt so much already, one more blow from Alex wasn't going to make a difference. "I'm just sorry," she lamented, "that we had to have this fight about Andrei."

"There is no fight. We have a saying in Russia. In love and war—"

"Everything's fair, right?" Leah snapped. She sniffed back her tears and rubbed her eyes. Flecks of dark mascara came off on the back of her hand. "Well, I don't believe it. I'm sorry about Andrei—but, Alex, he just isn't worth it," Leah blurted out.

Alex shouldered her tiny purse and started down

the stairs. "That is easy for you to say. He wants you. He kisses you."

"Oh, shut up!" Leah cried, and burst into a new round of tears.

Alex looked back over her shoulder and hesitated. "You and Andrei had a fight, is that it?" Alex sounded so cold, the tears dried in Leah's eyes.

"No," Leah said with deliberate calmness. "That's not it, Sorokin. I'm afraid our wonderful Andrei is a bit of a creep. He's a liar and a cheat." Leah's cheeks grew hot just remembering how he had leaned on her shoulder in the movie theater. "And I'm sorry that I, for one, got taken in by him."

"What are you talking about?"

"Alex, he's getting *married*."

Alex looked at Leah as if she were crazy. "What are you—"

"You don't have to believe me. Go out there." Leah pointed to the door. "Ask him. If you can work your way through the throng of well-wishers. The lucky girl's name is Claire."

Alex recognized the name instantly. "Claire DuParc!" Alex shook her head slowly. "Of all the nerve. He told me about her, Leah." Alex slapped her forehead and groaned. "He told me she was coming here to dance with him and with the company for several performances after the holidays."

"So that's who Diana meant." Leah would have to apologize to Diana first thing tomorrow.

Alex didn't hear her; she was puzzling out the chain of events. "He told me. He said she was his closest friend back in New York. He called her a friend, Leah—" Alex broke off and bit her lip. A tear rolled out of the corner of her eye. She wiped it away with an angry gesture.

"I know, it makes me feel dumb, too," Leah said, and sat down heavily on the concrete steps. "I thought he loved me," she added in a very low voice.

"Me, too." Alex leaned against the metal banister and looked up at Leah. "Did he actually tell you that?"

Leah was so glad at the moment he hadn't. Her friendship with Alex was worth a whole corps of Andrei Levintoffs. "No, he never came out and said that. He just was so—"

Alex continued for Leah. Her voice was dreamy and slow. "So warm, and he kissed me, and I thought—"

"It was the real thing!" Leah concluded with a catch in her voice. Then she heard herself and began to laugh. It started deep down in her chest, almost like a sob, but suddenly Leah was laughing harder than she had laughed in weeks.

Alex looked at her, stunned, then slowly her full lips stretched into a smile and she began laughing, too. She sank down onto the steps and held her sides. When she could breathe again, she said, "We—we were both so stupid. I never, ever, thought I would be this dumb—over a guy, Leah. A crummy guy."

"We almost lost it," Leah said, suddenly serious. "We almost stopped being friends. Every day in the classroom we compete for Madame's attention, we compete for roles, but so far we've always managed to stay friends. But the first guy that comes along—" Leah broke off. The whole idea was almost too scary to consider.

"I hate to say this. And you must not tell a soul I did," Alex warned. "But I do not think we were dumb. We are a little inexperienced with boys this way. And maybe we are young."

"There you are!" Andrei's cheerful voice boomed in the hall. He was standing at the foot of the stairs. But when the girls looked up, his eyes were full of concern. "My two favorite students, missing out on the gala, and crying—" His hand went out, and his finger traced the streaky trail of a tear down Leah's cheek.

She pulled back as if she had received a ten-thousand volt shock.

Andrei's high forehead creased in a frown. "What is happening here?" He looked from Leah to Alex and back to Leah again.

Both girls turned their heads away. A pulse in Leah's temple began throbbing.

"Is it what Pam said about Claire? That I will marry soon?" He sounded so patient, so gentle, so kind it made Leah sick.

"Well, what do you think, Andrei Levintoff?" she burst out. "You hold hands with me, you kiss me, you tell me how wonderful I look." Leah caught a glimpse of Alex out of the corner of her eye. "And you probably told Alex the same things, too. All this nonsense about loneliness and people touching—oh, Andrei, how could you?" Leah cried then, breaking down as much from the stress of the gala as from her disappointment with Andrei. Andrei reached to comfort her, but Alex stepped quickly between them. She gathered Leah in her arms and smoothed her shaking shoulders with her hands.

For a moment the only sound backstage was Leah's muffled sobs.

"Alex, I am so very sorry," Andrei's voice quavered. He stood up and leaned against the wall. "I did not mean for this to happen. I like both of you. You are my good friends. Alex, you have always been a friend to me. You are special—but," and he was very gentle as he said, "like my little sister."

Leah felt Alex's hand tighten on her shoulder. Leah straightened up. Andrei handed her a handkerchief. Leah stared at it a moment, then took it.

"Thank you," she murmured. She blew her nose, then raised her eyes to Andrei's. They were the saddest blue she had ever seen. "Oh, Andrei. I think you really mean what you've just said. But that doesn't make either of us feel any better."

"But I do not want you to cry, not like this. You really have made me feel less lonely." Again he reached for Leah. This time she took his hand and held it between both of hers. Touching him made her very sad. At that moment she knew she'd never be able to listen to Debussy again.

After a moment Leah sighed. "We'll get over it." Leah glanced at Alex. Alex had loved him longer, ever since she was eleven. Even if it was just a crush, it would take her more time to forgive him.

"Leah's right," Alex mumbled, not quite able to meet Andrei's eyes.

"So, now we begin again. All of us will be friends?"

Both girls nodded.

Andrei cheered and did a thrilling leap down

the last five steps, landing as soft as a cat on the ground. "I am glad. Because I want to go out tonight with my friends."

"Go out?" Leah blew her nose one last time and got up.

"Where?" Alex asked, reaching in her bag for her compact.

"To dance."

"Dance?" Leah eyed her aching feet.

"At a disco. I have not been to one here yet."

"But Madame Preston—" Alex warned.

"She says that tonight is a special night for three friends. My car, ladies, is right outside." He bowed and with a flourish motioned them toward the door. For the first time Leah noticed her rose, its petals browning at the edge, tucked into his lapel.

"But there are three of us; who will dance with who?" Alex asked, a hint of possessiveness in her voice.

"I will dance with both of you, even if I have to fight off an army of boys. Two such beautiful women might be dangerous." Andrei hooked Leah's hand through his left arm, and Alex's through his right. "I may have my hands full with my rivals." Then he added gallantly, "And if you were older, Claire would have her hands full of rivals, too!"

"She still might!" Alex commented wickedly. She winked at Leah behind Andrei's back.

But Leah didn't return the wink. She had just had the craziest thought. Alex's tea leaves *had* mentioned a handsome stranger. Wouldn't it be funny if tonight at the disco she and Alex were both to meet a couple of very nice strangers?

Andrei Levintoff might very well have some real rivals after all.

Leah laughed out loud.

"What is the joke? I do not understand," Andrei said as he led the way through the parking garage to the car.

"Oh, just—the future." Leah chuckled. "Crystal balls, tea leaves, and that sort of thing!"

GLOSSARY

Adagio.   Slow tempo dance steps; essential to sustaining controlled body line. When dancing with a partner, the term refers to support of ballerina.

Allegro.   Quick, lively dance step.

Arabesque.   Dancer stands on one leg and extends the other leg straight back while holding the arms in graceful positions.

> *Arabesque penchée.*   The dancer's whole body leans forward over the supporting leg. (Also referred to as penché.)

Assemblé.   A jump in which the two feet are brought together in the air before the dancer lands on the ground in fifth position.

Attitude turns.   The *attitude* is a classical position in which the working or raised leg is bent at the knee and extended to the back, as if wrapped around the dancer. An *attitude turn* is a turn performed in this position.

Ballon.   Illusion of suspending in air.

Barre.   The wooden bar along the wall of every ballet studio. Work at the barre makes up the first part of practice.

Battement.   Throwing the leg as high as possible into the air to the front, the side, and the back. Several variations.

Bourrée.   Small, quick steps usually done on toes. Many variations.

Brisé.   A jump off one foot in which the legs are beaten together in the air.

Centre work.   The main part of practice; performing steps on the floor after barre work.

Chainé.   A series of short, usually fast turns on pointe by which a dancer moves across the stage.

Corps de ballet.   Any and all members of the ballet who are not soloists.

Degagé.   Extension with toe pointed in preparation for a ballet step.

Developpé.   The slow raising and unfolding of one leg until it is high in the air (usually done in pas de deux, or with support of barre or partner).

Echappé.   A movement in which the dancer springs up from fifth position onto pointe in second position. Also a jump.

Fouetté. A step in which the dancer is on one leg and uses the other leg in a sort of whipping movement to help the body turn.

Jeté. A jump from one foot onto the other in which the working leg appears to be thrown in the air.

Mazurka. A Polish national dance.

Pas de deux. Dance for two dancers. ("Pas de trois" means dance for three dancers, and so on.)

Pas de chat. Meaning "step of the cat." A light, springing movement. The dancer jumps and draws one foot up to the knee of the opposite leg, then draws up the other leg, one after the other, traveling diagonally across the stage.

Penché. Referring to an arabesque penchée.

Piqué. Direct step onto pointe without bending the knee of the working leg.

Plié. With feet and legs turned out, a movement by which the dancer bends both knees outward over her toes, leaving her heels on the ground.

> *Demi plié.* Bending the knees as far as possible leaving the heels on the floor.

> *Grand plié.* Bending knees all the way down letting the heels come off the floor (except in second position).

Pointe work.   Exercises performed in pointe (toe) shoes.

Port de bras.   Position of the dancer's arms.

Posé.   Stepping onto pointe with a straight leg.

Positions.   There are five basic positions of the feet and arms that all ballet dancers must learn.

Retiré.   Drawing the toe of one foot to the opposite knee.

Rond de jambe a terre.   An exercise performed at the barre to loosen the hip joint: performed first outward (*en dehors*) and then inward (*en dedans*). The working leg is extended first to the front with the foot fully pointed and then swept around to the side and back and through first position to the front again. The movement is then reversed, starting from the fourth position back and sweeping around to the side and front. (The foot traces the shape of the letter "D" on the floor.)

Tendu.   Stretching or holding a certain position or movement.

Tour en l`air.   A spectacular jump in which the dancer leaps directly upwards and turns one, two, or three times before landing.

Here's a look at what's ahead in SECOND BEST, the fifth book in Fawcett's "Satin Slipper" series for GIRLS ONLY

"Hey, you don't look so good," Linda commented to Leah. "Do you feel all right?"

"I guess I don't," Leah answered. "Actually, I haven't felt right since the party last night. I had too much junk food," she lied.

"Tell me about it," Linda said. "I think I ate a whole bag of potato chips. What's up with you, Kay?"

"With me?" Kay took the last bite of her pie and washed it down with a sip of milk. "Nothing's up. What makes you ask?"

"I thought you might have hurt yourself in class or something," Linda stated matter-of-factly. "When I dropped by school on my way back here, I noticed you'd taken your name off the list of the competition."

"What?" several voices cried in unison. All heads turned toward Kay.

"Why did you do a dumb thing like that?" Alex asked bluntly.

"Oh, I think I'd look too much like a canary dancing the Swan Queen," the short girl joked. Then she paused just long enough to get everyone's undivided attention. "Actually—it's part of my plan."

"Plan?" Leah repeated. She had a funny feeling in

the pit of her stomach. Wasn't it Kay who had said something about doing everything possible to help Katrina stay in school?

Alex narrowed her dark eyes and studied Kay. "I have a feeling, Katherine Larkin, that you're about to drop on of your famous schemes on us."

"It's not a scheme," Kay retorted with dignity. Then she sat up a little straighter in her chair and struggled to look serious. "I figured we have to do all we can to help Katrina win this scholarship. If she doesn't win, she's out of SFBA. If I don't win—" Kay gave a nonchalant little shrug. "My pride takes one more pratfall and then I get up, dust myself off, and nothing really changes."

"So you decided not to compete to give Katrina a better chance?" Linda asked, amazed.

Leah sat down slowly and carefully placed the stack of dishes back on the table.

Kay just grinned. "You got it—and I'm going to do my best to get as many girls as I can to stay out of the competition." She rubbed her hands together and looked expectantly around the table. "Any volunteers?"

Leah's heart almost stopped beating. The other girls were probably going to hop on Kay's bandwagon to save Katrina. If Leah didn't, what would her friends think of her? Competing for the scholarship would seem like competing against Katrina.

Alex drummed her fingers on the table then leaned back in her chair. "I do not like this plan."

"What's it to you?" Pam said archly. "You can't compete anyway."

"It's not fair to Katrina, that's why," Alex said firmly.

Kay balked. "What's unfair about it, Alex?"

"It makes it seem as if without interfering—that is not the word—" Alex looked to Leah for help.

It took a moment, but Leah finally found her voice. "You mean it's like fixing an election—something like that." Once Leah uttered the idea aloud, she was glad she had come up with a reason to say no to Kay's plan. Fixing elections was wrong, and rigging competitions was wrong, too.

Alex's face brightened. "Yes, that's it. And maybe Katrina could win this prize *without* your help, Kay."

"But just last night you sounded pretty skeptical about Katrina's chances—and that's when we all thought the ballet was *Giselle*," Abigail pointed out.

"I know that," Alex conceded, "and she will have a tough time. But it—it just seems very wrong to me."

"It doesn't to me," Suzanne said. "I'll volunteer to take my name off the list, first thing tomorrow."

Abby flashed Kay a timid smile. "Before class I'll cross my name off, too."

Linda shook her head. "No." She gave an apologetic shrug. "Kay's idea is really generous, but I can't afford not to at least try for the scholarship. My uncle took out a loan to send me here, and it just wouldn't be fair to him if I gave up."

Kay grabbed Linda's arm. "You're absolutely right. And I think that anyone who needs the money should go for it." Kay and Linda traded smiles, and then both of them turned to Leah.

Leah shrank back in her chair. "I—I—" She couldn't tell them she had to compete, but she also couldn't lie. "I don't know what I'm going to do yet."

"Come on, Stephenson," Pam said suddenly. "I know what you're going to do. The same thing I'm going to do. Leah, the great Stephenson, is born to compete. She wants to be a star, just like I do. And the only way you get to the top is to go for the brass ring every time." Pam's tone was sarcastic, even taunting, yet she spoke with a passion Leah had never seen in her before. Looking at Kay with unveiled contempt, Pam declared, "*I* for one did not come to this school to make things easier for Katrina Gray. I came here to be the best ballerina there is, and nothing and no one is going to stop me. Being noble sounds good, but I think it's more important to win. It's not tuition that's at stake here. It's a career."

Pam shoved her chair and got up. "Leah knows all about that. Why don't you ask her what she *really* thinks about throwing this competition in Katrina's favor? Beneath that sugar-and-spice exterior, Leah's a fighter." Pam tossed her mane of red curls off her face and looked around the table at each girl in turn.

Leah cringed. Pam had sized her up so perfectly. How did Pam know her so well? How did Leah ever end up being on the came side as the one student in SFBA that she really despised?

ABOUT THE AUTHOR

Elizabeth Bernard has had a lifelong passion for dance. Her interest and background in ballet is wide and various and has led to many friendships and acquaintances in the ballet and dance world. Through these connections she has had the opportunity to witness firsthand a behind-the-scenes world of dance seldom seen by non-dancers. She is familiar with the stuff of ballet life: the artistry, the dedication, the fierce competition, the heartaches, the pains, and disappointments. She is the author of over a dozen books for young adults, including titles in the bestselling COUPLES series, published by Scholastic, and the SISTERS series, published by Fawcett.